Other Titles by Joe Cacciotti

Hurricane Cores the Big Apple

Hurricane Rocks Wisconsin

Coming Soon
Hurricane Strips Las Vegas
Hurricane Strikes Rhode Island
Hurricane Mashes Idaho
Hurricane Gold Rushes California
Hurricane Volunteers in Tennessee

HURRICANE
Rocks Wisconsin

joseph j. cacciotti

Marbry Books

Hurricane Rocks Wisconsin

By Joseph J. Cacciotti

Paperback Book: ISBN: 978-0-9847683-4-9

E-Book: ISBN: 978-0-9847683-5-6

Cover by Jennifer Tipton Cappoen

Published by:

 Marbry Books
P.O. Box 894
Locust Grove, Georgia 30248 USA
www.MarbryBooks.com

This book may be purchased from MarbryBooks.com, Amazon.com, and other retailers around the world.

Dedication

To my mother and father,
Irene Rusniak Cacciotti and Joseph Cacciotti,
for giving me the courage to always go after
what I believed in.

To a very special friend, Harold A. Schink,
who asked me for a special favor, and inspired me
to keep on writing.

To my wife, Diane,
my three daughters, Wendy, Stacy, and Jennifer,
and my son, Joel Curran,
for believing in me.

Chapter One

It was the last week of March, and the school day had just ended at Racine High. Next week was spring break. A playful lightheartedness filled the air, and bouts of laughter could be heard as the students began their walk home. In just ten more weeks, the schools in Racine, Wisconsin, would be ending another school year, and the books would finally close for the summer. Everyone was looking forward to warm weather, freedom, and happy days ahead.

Racine, Wisconsin, located just south of Milwaukee on Lake Michigan, has a population of around 90,000. It is a very close knit city for its size, and everyone in Racine always seems to band together in times of trouble. However, even this close-knit community wasn't ready for what was about to happen.

Jeff Pearson, John Anderson, and Kyle Jennings were walking home behind Julie Miles, Jessica Peterson, Susan Watkins, and Shirley Dupree. They were telling jokes and teasing each other with silly names.

"Hey, girls, what kind of bell doesn't ring?"

"We don't know, Kyle. What kind of bell doesn't ring?" Shirley asked.

"A dumbbell. Get it, a dumb bell?"

"You're crazy, Kyle. Where do you come up with such lame stuff?" Shirley retorted, rolling her eyes dramatically.

"Hey, what would you call a dog with no legs?" John asked.

"We don't know, John. What do you call a dog with no legs?" Julie answered as her eyebrows drew down.

"It doesn't matter. He wouldn't come anyway."

"That's a mean joke, John. You shouldn't make fun of dogs. I happen to like dogs," Julie retorted, her disapproval showing on her face.

"Relax, pint size," Kyle said to Julie. "Some of the best things come in small packages. Don't you agree?"

Julie Miles was blonde and very petite. She was only five feet two and weighed about ninety-eight pounds dripping wet.

Kyle Jennings was only five feet nine, but he was a jock. Wrestling was his specialty, and he was quick as greased lightning. He had just taken the state title in the 120-pound class.

"Hey, how do you get a one-armed man out of a tree?" Jeff asked, smiling.

"Don't know, Jeff. How?" Jessica asked back.

"Just wave at him."

Jeff Pearson was a track star. Tall and slender, he measured in at six feet and weighed almost 160 pounds.

Rounding out the trio of guys was Jeff's best friend, John Anderson. John was a little shorter at five feet eleven inches. He was a receiver on the football team and was built much bigger than he looked due to his weightlifting. His training gave him so much endurance that he could outrun just about everyone.

Jessica Peterson and Julie Miles were both blondes, and if not for their height difference, you would think they were sisters. People often mistook them for sisters due to the fact that they lived right next door to each other.

Susan Watkins, like her best friend Shirley, was a very smart student. She had dark brown hair and stood five feet eleven inches, pretty tall for a girl. An avid basketball and baseball player, her height was her advantage.

Straight "A" student, Shirley Dupree, stood five feet four at best. She was always the life of the party, forever playing jokes on everyone.

Shirley grinned, having hoped for an opportunity like this. With spring break on the horizon, she had planned for it.

Shirley nudged Susan and smiled. Opening her gym bag as she walked, Shirley slipped her hand into the zip-lock bag she had inside, and carefully withdrew three water balloons. Handing one to the other two girls, Shirley called over her shoulder, "Hey, guys, do you know how to cool off three hot-shot jocks?"

"No, how?" they answered together, giving the girls their full attention.

"Like this!" Shirley yelled, laughing. In one swift motion, the three girls whirled around and threw their surprises. It was over before the boys knew what hit them.

"Wha ...?" John jumped back and yelped as the cold water soaked through to his skin. "Good thing those balloons were little, or you'd have to run the rest of the way home!"

They all laughed, and Kyle made a grab for Shirley, but she danced out of his reach.

Unless they had practice after school for their different sporting activities, the group of friends made this pilgrimage every day of the school year, even when raining if it wasn't a downpour. Because they all lived near each other, it only made sense for them to walk together, and they had done it since elementary school.

Kyle lived right across the street from "the blonde twins." After the three of them dropped off the route, Jeff and John would continue on with Susan and Shirley to the 900 block of Arthur Avenue where all four of them lived.

While the girls were still snickering and the guys were wringing out their shirttails, a car pulled up alongside the guys and stopped. Jeff leaned down to see who was driving.

"Oh, hi, Fred."

"Hey, Jeff, you're looking a little damp there, buddy. You guys want to go to the movies with us?"

"Nice set of wheels, Fred. Where'd you get this?" John asked.

"It's my dad's new car. He's on a business trip. It's only a couple of years old, too! Isn't it a beauty? Can't believe he said I could drive it until he gets back," Fred answered.

"Wow. Really cool. Hi," John said, looking at the two guys in the back seat of the car.

"These are my cousins, Bobby and Sam," Fred explained. "They're moving here in a couple of months, and I've been showing them around." His cousins only nodded.

"So, what's playing at the movies?" Jeff asked.

"It's a double feature with Clint Eastwood," Fred said.

"Eastwood! He's one of my favorite actors." Jeff looked at John, who nodded in assent, then turned back to Fred, "Give us a minute to let the girls know, and we're in."

Kyle shook his head. "You guys go ahead, I've got some things I have to get done."

Jeff turned toward the girls who had kept walking and let out an exasperated sigh. Running to catch up to them, he asked, "Hey, girls, wait up! You okay walking home alone today?"

"Jeff, for heaven's sake, it's only five blocks! Sheesh!" Susan said as she rolled her eyes.

"Come on, you know you can't live without me," Jeff said with a grin. Susan took a swing at him, and he laughed, jumping out of the way. Then he and John got in the car with Fred and his cousins, and they sped off.

Kyle caught up with the girls, and they continued on toward their respective homes.

"Do you believe those two?" Susan said.

"Yeah, after all, we'll be seniors next year," Jessica said.

"Just think, girls, one more year and then it's off to college."

"Hopefully, we'll meet some more mature boys there," Julie sighed, rolling her eyes upward.

"You mean men, don't you, Julie?" Jessica clarified. Julie blushed and they all started laughing.

Kyle had been trying to ignore them, but they heard him snort in response to their conversation, and they all started laughing.

"I know it's a year away, but have you decided what college you'll be going to?" Shirley asked the other girls.

"Julie and I are planning to go to White Water," Jessica answered.

"You're joking, right? I'm applying to White Water, too," Shirley said.

"Well, girls, it looks like we'll all be going to the same college," Susan chimed in.

"Are you serious, Susan? You're planning to go there, too?"

Susan nodded, "Looks like we'll be spending the next few years still together."

"Good friends are easy to split up, but great friends stay together forever," Jessica said.

Laughing and giggling, the girls continued their walk home. When they reached Julie's and Jessica's houses, Kyle muttered, "See you," and headed across the street toward his house. After he left, the four girls stood talking for a few minutes in front of Jessica's house. Then Susan and Shirley said goodbye and headed on down the street toward home.

Susan and Shirley had just turned the corner when a beat-up, old blue van pulled up to the curb next to them. Thinking it was some of their school friends, the two girls turned to see who was in the van. Suddenly, the side door was flung open as four men wearing ski masks jumped out of the van and grabbed them.

"Hey, what's going on?" Susan yelled before being hit in the stomach with a blow that knocked the wind out of her.

Shirley managed to get out a loud scream before she was slapped across the face. The assailants moved swiftly, using duct tape to bind their hands behind their backs and to tape their mouths shut. Roughly, they were shoved into the van and followed in by the men. Neither girl could believe what was happening. One minute they were walking down the street, and the next, they were bound and gagged captives in a strange van. Tears ran down their faces as they looked at each other, scared, helpless, and unable to talk.

Questions raced through their minds, expressed only with their eyes. *Who are these men? What do they want with us? Where are we being taken?* The idea crossed Shirley's mind that this could possibly be a joke, but in her heart, she knew there was no way. No one would hurt them like that for a joke. This was serious. So what was going on? Kidnapping? Maybe something worse?

Kidnapping made no sense. They had nothing of value. Their parents were just average working people. She prayed it wasn't for worse.

The guys pulled off their ski masks, but it was really dark in the van, too dark for the girls to see them clearly. Although they couldn't talk to each other, they used eye contact to try to communicate. Slowly, they moved their eyes from side to side, hoping to get a glimpse of their abductors.

There just isn't enough light back here, Shirley thought as she realized all the windows in the van were painted. Her eyes grew wider as she tried to rock forward against Susan. There was no way they could see out.

A door separated them from the driver, but the small opening in it did not allow them to see out the front window. Susan and Shirley had no idea where they were being taken. Without being able to see outside, they would be unable to tell anyone where they were if they were able to escape.

Someone cracked the door open slightly and handed back two cans of beer. Susan caught a glimpse of the driver. He had sandy brown hair that came down to his shoulders. His nose was thin and pointy, and his face looked long and narrow. Susan tried to catch sight of a street sign, but the door was closed before they passed an intersection.

One of the guys turned on the light in the back and twisted sharply to see what was digging into his back. He pulled a small wooden box from behind him and threw it in the back of the van. In the silence of the van it was as loud as a shot when it hit the back door, and both girls flinched.

In the light, with their masks off, the girls got a clear view of their abductors' faces. Two of them almost looked like twins, with matching mustaches and goatees. *Same barber*, Susan thought somewhere in the back of her mind. Both had medium builds, and one had a tattoo of a spider on his arm. It was hard to tell how tall they might be. The other two looked like older teenagers.

Shirley couldn't take her eyes off one of the boys. She was staring a hole in him. Susan watched as he became uneasy and switched off the light. She began to wonder how many abductors there were. If the four who grabbed them were in the back with them and at least two more were up front, were there six guys? Just for the two of them?

Chapter Two

It seemed like hours before the van finally slowed, crossed over some bumps, and stopped. Hoods were drawn over the girls' heads, and then the side door opened. Susan was pulled out of the van, and she could tell Shirley was dragged out right behind her. They were shoved forward and up four steps where a hand abruptly stopped them, causing Shirley, who was following close behind, to bump into her friend.

They heard the squeak of a door being opened. The rougher of the younger men pushed them hard from behind. Shirley tripped over the threshold and fell to the floor. The kidnappers laughed, and both girls realized it was the first time the kidnappers had made a noise.

One of them yanked Shirley to her feet. Both girls were led into a room where they were grabbed roughly by their arms and pushed to their knees on the floor. Shirley's knee was burning, and judging from the sting, she knew it was bleeding. But that didn't worry her nearly as much as what might be coming next.

The girls' heads were suddenly pushed face first into deep cushions that felt like a couch. They were held there until they began to fight for air. Releasing them, their captors laughed as the girls gasped for a deep breath of air. Shirley was crying from the pounding pain in her knee and the sheer terror she felt. Susan could feel her heart pounding in her chest. *This is for real*, she thought. It was no joke.

The hoods were finally removed from their heads and the tape jerked from their mouths. They both flinched from the pain. It felt like it tore their lips off their faces. The tape on their hands was left in tact.

They both jumped when the kidnappers left and the door slammed behind them. They heard the van start up and drive away. The girls looked at each other with raised eyebrows wondering what was going on. Slowly, they looked around and saw that the villains had left them alone.

Both girls squinted as their eyes adjusted to the dim light in the room. It was a large open space with a fireplace in the middle of one wall. To the left was a door that probably led to the kitchen, and just to the right was a big open staircase.

Susan could sense that Shirley was not herself. She looked as if she had seen a ghost. Susan continued to look around the room. There were four big windows in this room, each boarded up tight. The only source of light was from nightlights scattered throughout the space.

Shirley's thoughts finally settled, and her mind returned to the situation at hand. Rolling over on the floor, she managed to sit up. Susan followed suit. Their hands were still taped behind them, and they knew they needed to get loose.

Susan spoke first. "Let's sit back to back and see if we can get this tape pulled off of our hands." They scooted around on their behinds until they were back to back.

Sitting upright, Susan was not able to find the end of the tape on Shirley's wrists using her fingers. She turned her body around and lay on her side facing Shirley's back, bringing her face close to Shirley's hands. Shirley's hands were cold from the lack of circulation. She managed to peel off a corner of the tape using her mouth and her teeth. After a few agonizing minutes, she used her teeth to try and rip the tape. She finally succeeded in getting it to tear. Rolling back into a sitting position she again scooted against Shirley's back.

With a few desperate tugs, she felt the tape start to tear. Then with three hard pulls, Shirley's hands were free. Shirley shook her hands to get the feeling back and removed the tape from Susan's hands.

All the windows were boarded up from the inside, and the handles to the outside doors had been taken off to prevent the girls from escaping.

"What's going on? Who are those guys, and why did they take us?" Shirley needed answers.

"I don't know, but we've got to find a way out of here before they come back!" Susan replied. "What's upstairs?"

"Let's check it out, shall we?" Shirley responded.

They raced up the staircase hoping to find a window they could climb through to escape. When they reached the top and the four closed doors, Susan said quietly, "You check those two, and I'll check these."

"I think we should stay together," Shirley replied. "There's no telling what or who might be behind them."

The girls approached the first door. Susan put her ear against the door to listen. "I don't hear anything."

She turned the handle and opened the door to an empty room. The windows were boarded up. "They sure like nightlights. They are everywhere."

"Maybe they are afraid of the dark." Shirley grabbed Susan's hand, "Let's check the next room."

The girls opened another door, revealing a huge bathroom equipped with a hot tub and two shower stalls.

"Where are we?" Susan asked.

"I'm not too sure, but I think I have been in this house before!"

"You're kidding, right?"

"No, it was before my mother divorced my dad and married my stepfather."

"I didn't know. I'm sorry about your bad luck."

"What bad luck? It was the best move my mother ever made. After my father lost his good paying job, he started drinking and beating my mother. She tried to stay with him and work things out, but when he started beating my brother Jimmy and me, she divorced him. He went to jail for putting my mother in the hospital and breaking Jimmy's arm. He hurt me as well," Shirley replied. "But you need to know one thing, Susan, Raymond may be my stepdad, but he is my *real* father. He's everything a father is supposed to be."

"Shirley, do you think your dad kidnapped us?" Susan asked.

"I don't think so. He is not due to get out of jail yet, and he doesn't even know where we live. Besides, why would he kidnap you?"

They continued exploring. Behind door number three, there was a queen size bed, and like the other rooms, the windows were boarded up. In the fourth room, they found an old computer on a small desk. Next to the desk was an old camera and a chair. The windows in this room were also boarded up.

"Look, more nightlights," Susan noted.

"At least the electricity works! We may need heat tonight," Shirley managed a small grin.

"I'm not planning on staying that long!"

"I wonder what's in here?" Shirley opened the closet door, and a videotape fell to the floor.

"What is that?"

"It looks like a VCR tape for that recorder over there. Maybe it's hooked up to the television on the desk next to it."

Shirley walked across the room. Leaning over, she found the switch to turn on the television. After they figured out how to work the player, they inserted the tape.

Susan and Shirley began to cry. What they saw on that tape looked like another girl being tortured by four men wearing masks. They heard one say, "Your parents thought we were kidding when we said if they didn't pay they'd be sorry."

Susan spoke first with fear in her voice, "We have to find a way out of this, Shirley. Our parents don't have any money. What did we happen to fall into here?"

"Let's go in the basement and see if we can find anything to tear the boards off the windows," Shirley suggested.

They made their way to the basement door and flipped the light switch. There was a little glow but not very much light. Considering what kind of lights were throughout the house, it had to be more nightlights. When they finally stepped onto the basement floor, they found out it was clean, no tools or rocks, no anything in sight that they could use.

"Well, Shirley, they made sure this place was clean before bringing us here."

Heading back upstairs, Shirley happened to notice something. She walked underneath the staircase, and there it was. They must have stuck that screwdriver into the two by four and forgotten it.

"Look at this. It doesn't look like they're perfect after all," Shirley exclaimed as she grabbed the screwdriver. When they reached the top of the stairs, she said, "Susan, listen for the van, I'll try to pry a board loose from the window."

Susan yelled, "Someone's coming!"

Shirley hid the screwdriver in her boot as they both sat down on the floor and waited for the worst. A key turned the tumbler, but only four figures came walking through the door.

"Well, aren't you ladies full of surprises? I didn't think you were smart enough to figure out how to untie each another. Not that it's a bad thing, mind you. You just saved us a little time.

"Now, I want you to sit down, and each of you write your parents a letter. Let 'em know you're still alive for now and won't be hurt, if they cooperate with us. Instruct them not to call the police or any private eyes. We'll call 'em in two days' time with instructions. If they follow them to the letter, we'll let you go. If they try anything else besides what we tell them, well, you'll find out later what will happen."

They threw them each a pad of paper and a pencil. Then he said, "After you're done, we'll go out and get you some food. We don't want anything to happen to you and possibly ruin our fun for later."

They did as instructed, and the four kidnappers were gone again. Soon after the van left, Shirley was back at work on the boards.

"Shirley, what's on your mind?"

"Nothing. I'm all right. Why would you ask me that?"

"That's the second time you froze when you saw that young boy. Do you know him?"

"I think I've seen him before, but I can't remember where. Enough with the talking. We have a lot of work to do."

"Shirley," Susan asked, "what do you think our chances are?"

"I think we have a good chance of getting out of here alive," Shirley replied.

"How can you be so confident?" Susan asked.

"My stepfather is an ex-Marine, and he taught me how to write in a certain way if I was ever in trouble," Shirley responded.

"What good does that do now?" Susan asked.

"Remember, I told you I thought I was here before? I think I know where we are, and I secretly put that into the letter. I just hope I did it right. It's been a while since I wrote one," Shirley said.

"A little praying won't hurt. I'll start now," Susan said.

"I just thought of something!" Shirley suggested. "They never asked us to address an envelope. How do they know where we live?"

"Good point, Shirley. They must either know us, or they've been following us for a while," Susan responded.

"I don't think so," Shirley answered back. "I better get back to work on these boards. Keep an ear on things in case they come back."

Susan smiled at her friend and then stood up and started walking around. She tried the front door. It didn't budge. She had all these bad images going through her mind, especially after seeing what they did to that other girl on the videotape. She went back upstairs into the bedroom and inserted the tape once again. She watched the action and noticed something strange. That girl never showed any fear and didn't scream as they pulled off her fingernails. Either she was already dead, or it was a fake, and they were supposed to find this tape to frighten them into doing exactly what they wanted.

Chapter Three

It was almost dinner time, and Shirley wasn't home from school. Shirley's mother, Connie Dupree, decided to call Susan's parents, Anne and Frank Watkins, to find out if Shirley was at their house.

"Hello, Anne. Is Shirley over there?"

"No, they never came home from school, and I was just about to call you to ask about Susan," Anne replied.

"It's not like Shirley," Connie commented about her daughter. "She always calls us if she's going to be late."

"Yes, and Susan's the same way," Anne added.

"I'll call Julie Miles, and see if they are over there. Maybe they don't realize how late it is," Connie told Anne.

"Alright, Connie. I'll call Jessica Peters, just in case she's there instead. Either way, I'll let you know."

They hung up and Connie dialed Julie's number. She answered after five rings. "Hello, this is Julie."

"Hello, Julie. This is Shirley's mother. Could you please tell her to come home? Supper is almost ready."

"She's not here, Mrs. Dupree. Shirley and Susan went straight home after we stopped at our houses. Don't tell me they never made it home!"

"Don't worry, Julie. We'll find them," Mrs. Dupree said. Her mind was racing as she hung up the phone.

"Raymond, Julie said they were walking right home after Jessica and Julie stopped at their houses."

Raymond replied, "I'm going to call the police." Just as he started dialing, there was a knock on the door. He paused to see who was there.

Connie went to answer the door, hoping it would be someone with good news. There was no one in sight, but a letter had been taped to the door. She quickly retrieved the letter and recognized the familiar handwriting as that of her daughter. As the read the letter, the color drained from her face, and she groped for something to hold on to. She was unable to move her eyes away from her daughter's letter. It was obviously Shirley's handwriting, but it must have been written under duress because of the many misspellings. Shirley was an excellent speller.

"What's the matter?" Raymond asked, something close to panic in his voice as he walked to her. Connie handed him the letter. By the time Raymond finished reading, Anne and Frank Watkins were at their door.

"They have my baby!" Anne cried out.

"They have Shirley, too," Connie said, almost in a whisper. She was trying to hang on to her emotions, knowing she needed to be in her right mind if they were going to get their daughters back.

"Whoever those bastards are, they have our children. We can't call the police, or they'll kill them! What can we do?" Frank Watkins asked, his desperation coming through in his voice.

Raymond Dupree's face suddenly lifted, and he answered, "I know someone, and he's just the man for this job."

Raymond and Frank went into the den and closed the door. They told the women to make some coffee. They had work to do.

"Frank, this guy's a bit unorthodox, but he knows how to get the job done."

"I don't care how he works as long as he kills those bastards."

"Your wish might be granted," Raymond responded.

Raymond took a black book out of his desk and started dialing. After four rings, a look of concern began to cover his face. He was hoping his friend was still around. After the sixth ring, someone picked up.

"Hello. This is Sam."

"Hey, Sam, old boy. I'm glad you're home!" Raymond said.

"Yes, okay, but who is this?"

"Raymond Dupree, Sam. It's been a long time, and I need your help."

"Raymond, old buddy, it has been a long time. But you sound worried.

20

What kind of problem could I help you with, Ray?"

Raymond turned on the speaker so Frank could listen in and then told Sam what had happened.

"Those bastards took our kids," Frank kept saying loud enough for Sam to hear.

"Settle down, and take a breath. What do you mean your kids were taken?"

"Sam, our teenaged girls didn't come home after school today, and we both just received ransom notes telling us 'no police' or they'll kill our girls," Frank explained.

"Ray, try and keep it together, brother. Don't do anything that might provoke them. As soon as we hang up, I'll be heading toward your house. By the way, Ray, what is your address?" Sam asked.

"554 Arthur Avenue. It's off of Kinzie Avenue," Raymond answered.

"Hold tight, Ray, I'm on my way. I should be there in a little over two hours. And, Ray, if they should call, try and record everything they say," Sam instructed.

"I'm sorry to call you, Sam, but I didn't know where else to turn," Ray apologized.

"Ray, don't lose it, and stop talking stupid. I'll be there in a couple hours, three at the most. I'll get them back safe, brother. That's what I do best," Sam encouraged as he hung up the phone. Before the phone hit the receiver, Sam was headed straight for his truck. He knew the longer he waited, the harder it would be to locate the girls.

Frank looked at Raymond curiously and then asked, "Are you two really brothers?"

"We are brothers in so many ways, not blood related, but brothers just the same."

Frank didn't understand, but now wasn't the time for that conversation. He decided to just let it pass for now. Besides, they had other more important things on their minds at this time.

Connie and Anne opened the door and walked in with a tray of coffee and sandwiches. The men shook their heads in a kind gesture and proceeded to sit down.

Connie was the first to break the silence, "Have you two come up with a plan yet?"

"As soon as Sam gets here, I'll feel a lot better," Raymond answered.

"Sam … you mean your buddy from the service? You haven't seen him for almost six years."

"Yes, one and the same," Raymond answered.

"What in the world can he do for us?" Frank asked.

"Do you remember reading about the man who saved that girl from certain death from those four kidnappers about two years ago? He brought her back home safe and unharmed. In fact, he also saved a Judge at the same time," Raymond responded.

"I vaguely remember that. Why do you ask?" Frank asked.

"Sam was the man who saved that girl. I think he's the best chance we have of seeing our daughters again alive," Raymond told him.

"Is he the one the papers called 'the Hurricane'?" Frank asked.

"Yes, and he certainly earned that name by destroying everything in his path that was necessary to get the job done. There is nobody else I'd feel more comfortable with getting our daughters back. We became very close to each other in the service. We watched each other's back like we were glued to each other. We made a pledge that no matter where we were after the service, if we needed any help, we wouldn't hesitate to call one another. I would bet my life on Sam, and I know he feels the same about me. Sorry, folks, you get me started talking about Hurricane, and I just can't stop," Raymond said.

"I can vouch for that," Connie responded and then added, "I just hope he gets here soon. I'm a bundle of nerves. I want my little girl back," she said with tears streaming down her face. Anne joined in with her own fresh tears flowing freely.

They all sat down, and waited anxiously for Sam's arrival. Raymond read the letter from Shirley again, and this time, his eye caught the errors in his daughter's spelling. He started smiling and went for the locked drawer in his desk. After shuffling a few things around, he pulled out his very worn code book.

"A code book? What are you going to do with a code book?" Frank asked him.

"I taught Susan that if she was ever in trouble and could get a letter to me, to use a few misspelled words every now and then to let me know where she might be. I noticed while reading her letter that she had a lot of

22

words spelled wrong. I have to put each misspelled letter on a piece of paper, which will, hopefully, spell out just where they are or might be."

"She could have misspelled them out of fear more than sending a secret message" Frank interrupted.

"Yes, Frank, maybe the big words, but her mistakes are in the smaller words. She's an A student when it comes to spelling, so I'm hoping she remembered what I taught her. Besides, I need to try to do *something*, rather than just sit here and wait," Raymond explained.

Raymond and Frank grabbed a pen and paper and started writing down the misspelled words. Time seemed to go much faster as they waited for the Hurricane to arrive.

Chapter Four

There was a loud knock on the door that jarred the household. Ray and Frank quietly approached the door together. Frank had the baseball bat ready as Raymond opened the front door.

"Put down your weapons!" Hurricane said. He was standing on the front stoop trying not to laugh at the sight of the two men.

"Sam? How in the world did you get here so fast from New York?"

"I was actually in Wisconsin, Ray, upstate a ways checking out Lambeau Field in Green Bay. I'm a diehard Packer fan. The folks up there are just great. I found out if you talk Green and Gold, everybody will talk to you. Racine was a lot closer than I thought," Sam answered.

"Oh, I didn't know I was calling your cell number," Raymond said.

"Do you remember Doug Stone?"

Raymond nodded his head yes.

"It was his daughter I had to rescue in Brooklyn, New York, along with Judge Grogan in Manhattan, and the mayor in Staten Island. I received this phone as a gift. I can get calls transferred from my house in Manhattan to anywhere in the United States. It sure comes in handy, especially like today," Sam said.

"I remember hearing something about that. I also heard you were shot."

"That was almost two years ago. I'm fine now. So you've been following my stories, have you?" Sam asked.

"When they smear it all over the front of the newspaper, it's kind of hard to miss," Raymond answered.

24

Connie and Anne entered the room. "Sam, these are our wives. This is my wife, Connie, and that is Frank's wife, Anne. We are all very grateful that you could come," Raymond told Sam.

"I wish we could have met under different circumstances, but I'm very happy to meet you," Sam said, shaking their hands.

"Enough of the small talk." Sam's adrenaline was rushing, and he was ready to get started on the case. "We have problems to solve."

"Yes, I'm glad to see you again, Sam. I, too, wish it was on better terms, but let's get down to business."

"Let me see the letters the kidnappers left on your doors."

"Your father taught you well, girl," Sam chuckled as he noticed the misspelled words in Shirley's letter. "You will be contacted in two days? Why would the kidnappers wait two whole days? Are they trying to cause more emotional stress? Or are they not so sure of what they are doing?" Sam pondered aloud. "Ray, have you decoded your daughter's letter yet?"

"Frank and I are about halfway through it. Would you care to join us?"

"I thought you would never ask." Hurricane smiled. He was not overly concerned about his ability to get the girls back safely. "We have two days to figure out where the girls are. Do I smell coffee?"

"I'll get it!" Connie called from the kitchen where she and Anne had been listening.

"These guys are not professionals," Hurricane noted.

"You can tell that just by a letter?" Frank questioned.

"If they were pros, that letter would never have arrived with easy words misspelled. That is a dead giveaway in this business. It's a very old tactic that's been used for years in the spy business," Hurricane explained.

They resumed reading and decoding the letter:

Hhigh mom and dad oover at Susan's house, uunder much stress, not really ssafe, where we are eeveryone in a bad mood. Bbefore you read this oonly you are to aadd up the rreal numbers.Ddad is not to eenvolve any police or we ddie. If you call uupp police we will be fforced to do things oonly against our will, uunder no circumstance no rrescue attempts must be mmade.

Eeveryone is to act nnormal don't worry now iinn no trouble.

Ssoon you will receive a kall with some iinstructions what to do. Hhow you react will determine Susaan and my fate. Ttoday we are safe sso please do as asked, bbefore I finish I llove both of youu, and eeveryone in the house. Bbe by the phone eeveryday help us get aabove this cloud, ttoday I am uupp in a dream. I'm havving a hard time being aable to write this letter. Nnever thought I'd be in this situation again, it feels like I've been here before. Love, Shirley

---

"She gave us some good clues. Now all we have to do is put them together," Sam said. "If you take the first letter of each misspelled word …"

"House boarded up," Frank interjected. "Four men in ski masks, blue beat up van … what am I missing?"

"Very good, Frank. You would have made a good spy," Sam said.

"The last line reads, 'Feels like I've been here before.' She's trying to tell us something. I can just feel it in the pit of my stomach. Or am I just grasping and hoping?"

"Always trust your gut feelings," Sam instructed. "Most of the time they are exactly right." Sam headed toward the front door.

"Where are you going?"

"I have a few things in my truck that might come in handy. Want to give me a hand bringing them in, or do I have to do all the work?"

Raymond and Frank hurried to follow Sam. "What could you possibly have in the truck that would help us?"

"Stuff," Sam smiled. "Here, grab these two duffle bags, Ray." Kneeling on the tailgate, he scooted a box toward Frank. Can you get this one? It has my computer equipment, so it may be heavy."

Sam grabbed two suitcases, and the three men went inside to set everything up.

Anne and Connie came to see what the men were up to. "Hurricane, if you need help on the computer, we work for the government," Anne informed Sam. "Connie works next to me, and she's also very good on the computer. We can help."

"I just might take you up on your offer. It's not too often I can find anyone capable of helping me, especially on this computer," Sam proceeded to open one of the suitcases. He pulled out what looked like a little pill container.

"Who has touched these letters?"

"Besides the five of us," Ray replied, "our daughters, and whoever dropped them off. Why?"

Sam didn't answer as he continued opening his little case. He took out a cloth and spread it over the table. He laid the letter on top of the cloth. Then he took a small syringe and sprinkled some solution on the corners of the paper. "Someone turn off the lights and close the curtains," he instructed.

When the room was dark, several sets of fingerprints materialized. Sam pulled out a pocket camera, took several shots, and removed the memory card. He inserted the card into his computer and clicked to a web site. "Now we will see whose fingerprints, besides ours, are on these letters. This will take a few minutes, so let's work on decoding this letter." Turning to the women, Sam said, "Connie, how well do you and Anne know your neighbors?"

"Very well. Why do you ask?" Connie answered.

"I'd like the two of you to go around and ask your neighbors if they recall seeing an old beat-up blue van driving through this neighborhood in the last few days or so. We might get lucky. Maybe someone has seen it or the driver."

"We can do that, "Anne answered.

"It will make us feel like we're helping and not just standing on the sidelines," Connie added.

"You take that side of the street," Anne pointed, "and I'll take this side." The ladies left in a hurry with a plan to gather information that might help Sam find their daughters.

"Frank is right," Sam said. "There is something we are missing. The last line of Shirley's letter has to mean something."

"She must have been pushed to hurry and didn't code the last part," Frank suggested.

"There is only one misspelled word and it goes with the word 'van' that is the part of the message before the last line: Nnever thought I'd be *in this situation again, it feels like I've been here before."*

"Maybe this part is not written in code. Maybe it is literal. Maybe she is somewhere she has been before," Sam told them.

The men continued to uncover clues for the next half hour.

Anne and Connie burst into the house excited and talking at the same time. "They've seen the van! They heard tires squealing!"

Sam whistled and waved his hand, "Ladies, please, one at a time!"

Anne started again, "Julie Miles and Jessica Peterson were the last two to see our girls. After they went to their respective houses, Susan and Shirley were seen heading toward home. Julie and Jessica both heard tires squeal shortly after leaving Susan and Shirley before they had turned the corner of Kinzie Avenue, and they both saw a beat-up blue van speeding up the street."

"Julie said she believes the license plate started with the letters "BAD" but couldn't read the rest because it was going too fast," Connie added.

"Great. As soon as I run these fingerprints, I'll try the plate numbers. Maybe we'll get lucky," Sam said. "Did anybody else see or hear anything?"

"I wish those boys had walked them home like they always do," Connie mumbled.

"What boys, Connie?" Sam was unfamiliar with the girl's routine. "Who are you talking about?"

"Jeff Pearson, John Anderson, and Kyle Jennings always walk home with the girls, and today of all days, one of their friends and his two cousins stopped in his dad's car on the way home and asked the boys to go to the movies with them," Anne answered.

"Do these boys live around here?" Sam asked.

"Yes, Jeff lives in the brown house over there," Connie said as she pointed toward the house two doors down and across the street. "John lives almost directly across from us, and Kyle lives across from Julie's and Jessica's house, but Julie said Kyle didn't go with the boys. Why?"

"Have you told the boys what has happened?" Sam was curious.

"No one answered either door when we knocked," Anne answered.

"This may have been a planned attack," Sam suggested.

"What are you saying? Do you think they were part of it?"

"I don't think they knew a thing, but I bet their friends who picked them up were a part of it. How would they know the girls would be alone on this day?"

"Especially when everyone knew the boys were always with them," Frank was starting to get the picture.

"Yes, I think this was a well-planned scheme," Sam added, "but they didn't know about one big problem facing them."

"What would that be?" Raymond sprang to life with hope.

"The Hurricane!" Sam remarked. Everyone managed to laugh in spite of the circumstances.

Suddenly, the computer started beeping. Sam walked over and picked up the pictures and fingerprint forms from the printer. He started sorting through them.

"Hmmph," he smirked. "I think we have a couple of faces to go with these prints. Do you remember seeing any of these guys around here in the past few days?" Sam passed around the pictures.

Anne spoke first, "Hey, I've seen this one by the school several times. I don't know if he's a student or an employee. I don't know the other man."

"Neither do I," Connie added. "The letter said there are four men. That is if we have figured Shirley's codes correctly. We only have two sets of prints, what about the other two men involved?"

"You have to have a little patience, Connie." Sam assured. "We know who two of them are. All we have to do now is find them."

Frank had been standing by the window. When he heard car doors close outside, he peered out the window. "The boys are home from the movies!" He hurried to the door where he leaned out and shouted, "Jeff, John, can you come here for a moment?"

When the boys entered the house, they immediately saw the two women crying. Jeff nervously responded, "What's wrong, Mrs. Watkins?"

"Our girls never made it home today, guys," Frank informed them.

"What? That's impossible!" Jeff said.

"Please don't clown around like this, Mr. Watkins." John hoped they were teasing.

"I wish it was a joke," Raymond told him.

"But we aren't laughing," Sam came to the forefront.

The boys turned serious. "What happened to them?"

"All we know is that a beat-up old blue van with four guys inside kidnapped our daughters as they were walking home. We were hoping you might be able to help us make sense out of this," Mr. Dupree explained.

"Your friend who picked you up this afternoon, has he ever asked you to go with him before?" Sam asked.

"No, this was the first time he has ever asked us to go anywhere with him," John answered. "Who are you?"

"Who I am is not important now," Sam said sternly. "What is important is that you tell us the names of all the friends you were with today?"

"You don't think they had anything to with this, do you?" Jeff asked.

Sam went into his detective mode. "Before I answer your question, let me ask you," Sam started, "how many times have the girls walked home alone without you guys by their side?"

"I don't think we've ever let them walk home alone. So how did the kidnappers know we weren't with the girls today?"

"Bingo! You would make a good detective, Jeff. You caught on fast," Hurricane said.

"Jeff, let's go ask our friends a few questions!" John was quick to offer.

"Hold it!" Sam said, "We have enough worries with the two girls gone. We don't need to have you guys end up missing, too."

"Wait, you never told us your name. Just who the hell are you?" John was getting angry.

"This is my long lost brother," Raymond proudly spoke up. "I haven't seen him in almost six years. May I introduce you to the Hurricane?"

"You're that guy from New York?" John's voice changed to excitement.

"Now, gentlemen," Sam said, regaining control of the conversation, "what are the names of your friends?"

"We don't know their last names, but we know where they hang out," Jeff said.

"We can take you there now!" John offered.

"Can you boys be up and ready to go tomorrow morning by six a.m.?"

"Yes, but why not take them now?"

"We'll have a better chance of catching them at home tomorrow morning than we would tonight. Besides, if they party all night, they'll be in no mood to fight back when we surprise them in the morning. And that way, maybe no one gets hurt. Tomorrow the Hurricane will rock Wisconsin."

Chapter Five

At six a.m., the alarm clock was blaring, just as planned. Raymond and Frank were up and ready by six-fifteen.

"Hey Ray, where's Sam?"

"If I know Sam, he was up long before the birds started singing."

As they came down the stairs, the aroma of coffee filled the air. Sam was in the kitchen sipping on a cup and packing his vest.

"Sam, what time did you wake up?"

"Same time I always wake up, Ray. Four thirty every day. When I have something pressing, I like a lot of peace and quiet to clear my mind before I get down to business, and besides, somebody here had to make the coffee."

Anne and Connie came walking into the kitchen, "I thought I smelled the coffee brewing."

"Come on over, ladies, and join us," Sam said.

"Sam, I heard you pacing the floor early this morning. Is there something bothering you?" Connie asked, just before they sat down at the kitchen table with the guys.

"I just hope those boys are on the up and up with us. I'd hate to think they were a part of this scheme."

"You don't have to worry about John and Jeff. They're almost like brothers to these girls. They've known each other for the past ten years, if not longer," Connie said.

"I'd have to agree with Connie about these boys, Sam. They're practically like family in our houses."

31

Sam still seemed a little worried as he looked at his watch.

"Don't worry, Sam, they will be here soon," Anne said. Just as she finished saying the words, the door opened and Jeff and John came in.

They froze when they saw Sam dressed in all of his apparel. He had on his army shirt and camouflage pants, but that wasn't what they were looking at. It was the weapons he was wearing—three holsters holding two .357 Magnums and a semi-automatic, 16-clip Lugar. He also had what looked like a sawed-off shotgun hanging by his hip, along with additional clips. He carried three extra straps with additional ammo for all three guns strapped around his chest, plus a few knives, and what looked like eight-point ninja stars. He was looking for answers, and they were betting he wasn't about to come up empty.

Sam asked Jeff to hand him his long overcoat. When Jeff picked it up, he couldn't believe how heavy it was. Sam nodded thanks, and when he put it on, Jeff saw the steel plates sewn into the chest area.

Loaded with all of his gear, Sam, the two fathers, and the two boys hopped into Sam's truck. John was in the front seat giving instructions on where to go. The vehicle was so quiet you couldn't tell if it was running. They arrived at 1124 North Memorial Drive and surveyed the house. Sam was about to exit the vehicle to check things out, but John stopped him. "Hold it, Mr. Hurricane. One of the cars is gone."

"What do you mean, gone?" Hurricane asked. "Maybe he parked it in the garage."

"No! He always parks in front," John answered.

Sam closed the door quietly and decided to wait a few minutes. Within five minutes a truck pulled into the driveway and stopped. Four guys stepped out carrying bags of fast food and drinks in their hands.

"Are those the guys?" Sam asked.

"That's Fred, but I don't know those other three guys. I've never seen them before," John answered.

"You don't think they're holding the girls here, do you?" Frank asked.

"Maybe we'll get lucky and find out who really has the girls. I'm betting they know something," Sam said, and then added. "Well, let's spoil their breakfast, shall we fellas?"

When John and Jeff made a move to exit the truck, Sam stopped them and said, "This is our play, boys. I don't want them knowing how we found out about them."

Jeff asked, "What if we go in first, just to make sure the coast is clear?"

"This isn't a game, son, you could get seriously hurt and maybe even killed. I couldn't live with that," Sam replied.

"We can't just lay back and do nothing. We feel it's our fault the girls are in this mess," interjected John.

"Alright, but when it gets serious in there, you two had better exit as fast as you can, and don't look back. Here's five dollars for each of you. Catch a bus back home, and wait for us," Sam responded.

They nodded their heads in agreement, hurried across the street trying to act nonchalantly, and entered the house. Within a few seconds, they were escorted out the door they had just entered. John and Jeff nodded their heads in a yes motion to let Sam know they were in there.

"Well, at least the boys are safe." Sam breathed a sign of relief. "Let's go, men. Raymond, you and Frank go around back. Make sure nobody leaves this party, and be prepared in case I need your help."

After waiting about ten minutes, Hurricane knocked on the door. The man who opened the door was looking down the barrel of a shotgun. John and Jeff watched from across the street as Hurricane entered the house. They couldn't wait as they ran back across the street, stopping at the window just in time to hear.

"Who the hell are you?"

Looking into the slightly opened window, John and Jeff saw Hurricane standing in the middle of a group of five guys, and they heard Sam say.

"I'm either your best friend or your worst enemy. How you answer my questions will determine which one you are."

"You don't have to force your way in here with that cannon just to ask us a few questions, pal," the big guy with the tattoos said.

"What might your name be, friend?" Sam asked.

"Steve, but who are you calling 'friend'? I don't know you yet."

"All in good time, Steve. Now, would any of you boys know anything about two high school girls getting kidnapped off the street yesterday?" Sam asked.

"Why, are we suspects? If so, you're free to look around," Steve said. "There ain't no girls here."

"I never said you were suspects," Sam answered. "However, someone did pick four of you out from some photographs. We are checking out leads, that's all. So, if you didn't take them, maybe you happened to see who did?"

"Sorry, pal, but we never seen no blue van snatching nobody," Steve answered.

"I never mentioned anything about a blue van, pal, so maybe you better tell me what you know!" Sam demanded.

"I'm not telling you nothing, copper!" Steve answered back, a sudden scowl covering his face as he realized his mistake. "You're outnumbered here, so why don't you just leave before you feel some real pain."

"I've already told you I'm not a cop." Sam's voice lowered almost to a whisper. "You really don't know who you're dealing with here. So, why don't you save yourself and your pals a lot of pain and medical bills and just answer my questions without any difficulty?" Sam asked and then added, "If I have to ask you again, I will not be as nice as I am now."

"I'll give you this much. You got a lot of guts coming in here alone and demanding anything from us." Steve stood up and approached Sam. "But you won't be walking out without help."

"I tried to be nice, but if you don't want nice ..." Sam moved as quickly as a cat and grabbed Steve by the throat. "Can't hear you, Steve. You have to speak up? Cat got your tongue? Oh, pardon me. I have your throat. You don't sound so tough now. In fact, I could kill you right now, but I wouldn't get the answers I'm looking for. Now, I'll just take you with me, and if you die telling me anything, I'll be back for your friends. Wait a minute, I'll just take your friends with me now, too. That will save me a lot of time," Sam said and then spun Steve around and tied his hands behind his back with a zip tie. "Now, who's next?"

"You aren't so tough, cop. I'll kick your teeth in," said another of the young men as he stepped toward Sam.

Sam spun and gave him a round house kick square in the mouth. He came up spitting teeth. When he charged again, Hurricane spun and kicked him in the back of his head, knocking him out. "Who's the next tough guy?" Sam asked.

A tall, wiry young man stood up and started throwing spin kicks and karate thrusts as he approached the Hurricane. He attempted an axe handle kick, in which he brings his leg straight up and down trying to dislocate a shoulder. When his leg was up, Sam squatted underneath, hitting him so hard in the family jewels that it took him right off his feet.

The last two guys came after Hurricane at the same time. Sam spun fast, hitting both of them on the sides of their heads. With a look of shock, they once again came after him. He stood still in the middle of the two men, and when they struck at him, he moved so fast they hit each other. Sam was done playing with these guys. He squatted and moved fast, swinging his leg and snapping one of the assailant's knees. The other one gave up instantly. They immediately put their hands behind their backs. Sam approached and tie strapped their hands before he called out, "Frank, Raymond, would you bring the truck around to the front? We have some questions to ask these fools."

When the truck was out front, Sam took the three who couldn't walk and tied them on top of the luggage rack.

"Sam, if you pass a squad car, he will definitely pull you over, my friend," Raymond said.

Sam took a cover out of the truck and covered the three men on top of the roof. By the time he was done tying up the cover, you couldn't even tell anything was up there. "Happy now, Ray? Can we get going now?" Sam asked with a little smirk on his face.

The other two were put into the far back seat with Frank. Raymond was in the middle seat holding a gun, just in case they tried any funny business.

Jeff and John must have hightailed it back home. They were nowhere to be found.

"What are we going to do with these guys?" Frank asked.

"Raymond, remember when we were in Korea and what they did to their prisoners?"

"Sam, you don't mean the broken toe torture?" Raymond answered.

"I forgot about that one, Raymond. I was thinking the skin head torture," Sam answered.

"You don't mean where they skin a guy's head and pour salt on his open wound do you?" Raymond asked.

They noticed their two prisoners in the truck were starting to sweat, just from hearing what they might be facing.

"I'm talking about the torture they learned from the Japanese back in

World War II," Sam said.

"Oh, you mean the bamboo stalks pushed up their fingernails?" Raymond asked.

"That's the one, Ray. Not too many guys made it past the third finger, if you remember," Sam answered.

"In fact, Jesse Richards lost two of his fingers after they pushed them up past his knuckle," Raymond mentioned.

"Yes. That reminds me ... after we are done here, I'd like to go visit Jesse and see how he's doing after all these years," Hurricane said.

"Maybe I'll go with you, Hurricane. I always liked him. In fact, he saved my butt a couple times in those days," Raymond said.

"Are there any vacant buildings around here we could use," Sam asked.

"Yes, there's an old barn not too far past the highway that we could use. I'll point the way." Raymond said.

"Let's go, Ray. This is when the fun begins," Sam said.

"Hey, Hurricane, how long were you in the service?" Frank asked.

"Six years, Frank. Six long years," Sam answered.

"If you didn't like it, why did you stay in that long?" Frank asked.

"I was given a choice of four years in prison or six years in the Army for doing something stupid in my youth," Sam answered. "I do admit that it was probably the better of the two evils. Who knows, I may have ended up in prison for life. Now, I have my own established business as a private investigator and the instinct of knowing how to track people down. Besides, I made a lot of very good friends in the service. We were like a family of brothers. It was hard to leave."

"Hey, Hurricane, not to change the subject, but where did you get this Land Rover?" Raymond asked.

"It was a going away present from the Army," Hurricane answered.

"Now, who do you think you're talking to, my friend? You might have talked them into one of the older models, but this one has the extra extended base for your third seat, plus the extra long trunk space. They were just coming out with this model when you left. Someone must have owed you a big favor," Raymond said.

"I must confess, Ray. You're right. I did buy a Land Rover from the service. It wasn't my fault they sent me the wrong one. But who am I to complain?" Sam said.

"I believe that part, but now tell me what it cost you?"

"I could never pull anything over on you, Ray. Alright, it cost me my entire army chest of smokes," Sam said.

"How did you collect a whole chest full of smokes?" Raymond asked.

"Since I don't smoke, whatever I won playing cards or getting free from the service, I put them into my army chest. I thought they might come in handy eventually. As you can see, I was right. Besides I had to rejuvenate a few things in this truck before it was ready to go. I replaced the regular suspension springs with some very tough and durable ones, including adding a few hiding places to haul my tools around in. A friend of mine worked on making the engine purr like a kitten. I'm not sure what he did, but it was worth every penny I paid him. It will go from 0 to 60 in five seconds flat. And my tires will stand up to any kind of heat or cold climate," Hurricane said.

"Why would you need such a big vehicle, Hurricane?" Frank asked.

"As you can see, Frank, in my line of business, I never know how much space or what kind of tools I might need. So I compromised on both accounts. Besides, wait until you see a few of my toys, and then you will understand," Hurricane replied.

Chapter Six

There it is, Sam!" Raymond said, pointing toward a barn out in the middle of nowhere.

"Where are we, Ray?"

"We are right between Franksville and Raymond, little suburbs of Racine County. It's nice and quiet here."

"Perfect spot, Ray, nice and secluded," Sam said. "Hey, Frank, could you help me get a few things out of the truck?"

Frank slipped out of the back seat and, along with Sam, grabbed the handles of the army chest and carried it into the barn. Raymond brought in the two punks from the back seat and sat them down in the corner on some hay bales.

"If you boys are smart, it will be a lot less painful to tell us *now* what you know because, by the time Hurricane gets done with you, I can guarantee you that it'll take a very long time to heal," Raymond said.

Sam and Frank brought in the other three guys from the top of the truck. The guy with the missing teeth was strung up from a beam in the barn with his toes barely touching the ground.

Raymond took the guy with the broken leg over by the wagon wheel.

"Wrap his arms through the wheel spokes like they did in Korea, Ray," Sam instructed.

Raymond knew what the Hurricane wanted as he wrapped his arms so his elbows pushed straight out in front of his body. He was twisted in a very awkward position.

Sam pulled Steve up with his powerful hand wrapped around Steve's neck. Sam figured he was the big tough guy of this pack, since he was the first one who tried to attack. Raymond brought over a chair, and Sam slammed him down. They tied him up with duct tape. His arms were taped with the palms of his hands up, and then his legs were taped to the legs. They threw a couple of ropes over the beams fastening them to the chair, so he could be hoisted up in the air.

"I don't know who left these chairs behind, but they will surely come in handy," Sam said.

Hurricane walked over to check on the others, the toothless man was hanging straight down, his toes barely touching the floor. The third guy with the broken leg looked like he was in pain with his arms stretched between the wheel spokes. His elbows were being hyper-flexed in an awkward way. The other two were brought in and seated on some hay bales, their hands still tied together, and now additionally tied to a tall stack of bales behind them.

Sam walked around surveying the work, and shook his head in approval. He noticed the men looking at each other and studying how they were tied up. Reaching into the pocket of his trench coat, he pulled out a long screwdriver, and a pair of pliers, along with a little three-pound hammer. "This will do for starters," he said and then proceeded to talk to his captives.

"Now, gentlemen, as you can see, I'm not a cop. If you would like to avoid a lot of pain, it's simple. Just tell us where the girls are, and we will drop you off at the police station safe and sound. If not, sooner or later, you'll tell us anyway. I hope you choose the later, it's been a while since I had this much fun," Sam grinned.

One of the guys started yelling, "You can't do this. We have rights. We will have you arrested."

Before he could get another word out, Sam spun and threw the screwdriver. It found its mark as the guy screamed. The screwdriver was sticking straight out from his knee.

"Does anyone else have any complaints, gentlemen?" Sam walked over, and jerked the screwdriver out of his knee. He screamed louder than before and the blood saturated his jeans. Hurricane walked over to the man hanging from the beam who had his teeth knocked out.

"I don't suppose you know anything, right, amigo?" He spat bloody saliva from his mouth at Hurricane. "You know it doesn't look right with your front teeth missing and the rest still in place, I'll have to remedy that."

Sam took out the pliers, prying and fixing them into the unwilling mouth. He pulled, and after the third tug, two more teeth came out. "Look there, only two more teeth. I bet I can do better this time. Maybe I'll try the bottom where there seem to be more teeth to grab onto." With that said, he did as promised. "You have or had some very strong teeth. I bet you brush every day," Hurricane said as he pulled three more teeth from his lower portion. "That's better. Now you're more in uniform. I'll let you rest a while. Just hang around, and I'll be back later. I can't leave all your friends out of all this fun," Hurricane said.

Hurricane walked over to the man with the broken leg and said, "If you tell me were the girls are, I'll get you to a doctor. Man, that really looks like it hurts!"

"Those guys will kill me if I tell you anything," he answered back.

Sam took out the little hammer and smiled. "My friend, this is going to hurt you real bad." As he walked over to the man tied on the wheel spokes, he swung that hammer, hitting the man in the other leg. He let out a scream as his leg nearly folded in half. Sam was still smiling as he asked, "Now would dying be as bad as what I'm going to be putting you through? Hold that thought. I'll be back."

Sam walked over to the two guys tied to the hay bales and said, "I hope you boys are smarter than your buddies because if I don't hear something soon, it just won't matter if you live or die. I'm only going to ask this question two more times and if nothing is settled, I'll leave you boys tied up for the animals to feast on." Then Hurricane looked right at them. "Where are the girls?"

"We don't know, mister. Honest!"

Hurricane picked up the big screwdriver. He held it like a knife as he approached them and raised his arm as if to strike. His eyes looked like he could kill. When he appeared ready to strike, one of the boys lost control of his bladder and wet himself. "Are you ready to talk, or should I give you a reason to get a new kneecap?"

"If we tell you what we know, will you let us go?"

"You better not tell them anything, Sam, if you know what's good for you," Steve shouted. Hurricane took note of Sam's name but said nothing.

Turning his attention toward Steve, Hurricane almost hissed at him, "I was going to save you for last, but since you insist, I'll quiet you up now. I know you aren't about to say anything, so why waste my time asking you a question."

Sam walked over to his army chest, and as he opened it up he looked toward Steve and said sternly, "I figured you were the one who knew what I wanted to know, so I have something special planned for you." When Sam turned he was holding a ten pound sledge hammer in his hands. "This may look like a sledge hammer, but it's also a great tool for crushing toes. You will have ten opportunities to tell me what I need to know … if you're as tough as you think and make it that far. And should you make it that far, then I'll smash your fingers. And then … well, a smart guy like you should be able to figure out the rest."

Hurricane removed Steve's shoes with his knife, and how he cut off those shoes without cutting the foot was amazing. Frank, Raymond, and Hurricane raised Steve's chair in the air by pulling the ropes and securing them around a big beam. Steve was just hanging there, helpless as a baby, as Hurricane walked up next to him. "You know what I want to hear, so I won't even ask. I'll just start smashing toes, and when you want to talk, just tell me," Hurricane said.

Hurricane walked around behind Steve, who wondered why he was raised into the air. He forgot about the other hammer Sam had used before, until both hammers smashed into his little toe. With no warning at all, he crushed the small toe. It looked like a piece of raw meat hanging there.

Frank didn't think Hurricane would do it, but now he knew he was out to find those girls. Sam raised the hammers once again and stepped up to the second toe. He looked at Steve, who must have been in shock, but he woke up screaming after Hurricane smashed the next toe. Hurricane paid no attention to the screams as he positioned himself for the third toe.

"No, wait, I'll tell you what I know. Just don't smash any more toes, please!" Steve cried.

"I'm listening," Sam said.

"I don't know who the guys are that kidnapped those girls. They just paid us to keep the boys busy, and we didn't exchange names. We didn't even know what they wanted with them. We did it for the money. They told us if we said anything they'd kill us, and that no harm should come to us because no cops would be involved," Steve said.

"Would you be able to point them out from a photograph?" Hurricane asked.

"I don't know if I could," Steve said. Just as Hurricane positioned himself by the foot, he yelled, "But I could describe what he looks like, if you want to sketch him out."

Sam eased up, wrapped a towel around the foot, and left him dangling there. He picked up his phone and dialed a number. "I need you," he spoke into the phone. After giving instructions on where to find them, he hung up. "When my contact gets here, you tell that person what he looks like, and if it pans out, we'll be back to untie you. If not I'll be back to finish the job I started," Sam said.

"We were told that nobody would be involved. Just answer us one question: who are you?" Steve asked.

Within a half hour, a helicopter landed in the field in front of the barn. A very huge person jumped out and headed toward the barn. He stood at least six foot ten inches, and with his gear on, he looked like a bull elephant. Hurricane met him at the door and explained what was going on. He started to laugh as he approached Steve. Then he saw the blood from the foot and asked, "How many did it take this time, Sam?"

"He's not as tough as he thinks. It only took two before he broke down," Sam answered.

"Jason, this is Steve. Steve has a face he would like you to draw, maybe even two or three. He's trying to save his life, as well the lives of his friends."

"Who is that guy?" Steve asked Jason when Sam turned away.

"Gentlemen, they call him 'Hurricane'!" Jason answered. "In fact, you are all so lucky to still be alive. You must have something he needs really bad. You're smart to answer his questions, but heed my warning. If you give him the wrong information or are too late with what he wants, there is no place on earth you could hide to escape what he will do to you. He makes the devil himself look tame."

Suddenly, young Sam yelled from the hay bales across the room, "You're out of your district. You can't touch us!" He would quickly find out that you shouldn't get the Hurricane mad.

"There is only one problem with that," Hurricane said as he walked toward young Sam. "When I found out your name was the same as mine, I kind of liked you. Now I think you're like Steve over there, a scumbag."

Hurricane brought the screwdriver down right into his kneecap. Young Sam bellowed in pain. "By the way, I have a license to go wherever I wish to fight scumbags like you. Now, you boys just stay right here in pain while we check out your stories. Don't go anywhere. We'll be right back. I promise."

"We can't just go and leave them like this," Frank said.

"Relax, Frank. Just remember they have your daughter or know the people who do. That is what we are trying to find out. If it checks out, they are free to go," Sam said as he brought a laptop computer out of his army chest and turned it on. "Besides, we aren't going anywhere. We will check them out right here." Sam dialed a number that went somewhere into Washington, D.C. He scanned the artist's sketch Jason gave him of the supposed suspect, and uploaded the electronic file through his special hookup on his laptop.

"I'd like to know where you get all your toys, Sam," Frank spoke out.

"That isn't a toy, Frank," Raymond interrupted. "Those are tools of the trade. This is what makes Sam the best in the business, and he's prepared for almost anything."

Within a span of ten minutes, Sam received back a wanted poster with a picture of the same man that Jason had sketched from Steve's description. He was wanted in ten states for kidnapping and murder, and among a few other traits, his hands were registered as lethal weapons. His last known location was Cleveland, Ohio. When Sam saw that, he immediately picked up his phone and made a call. "Chet, Sam Rufus here. I think I have someone in Wisconsin who may interest you."

Sam explained what he was into, and then asked if there was anything he should know about this guy they were after. When he finished his conversation and ended his call, he turned and addressed the two fathers of the kidnapped girls, "Gentlemen, this is going to get real messy. So if you want to back out, I will not hold it against you."

"What do you mean, messy?" Frank asked.

"Seems like this guy is with a group of very bad men, they kidnap young victims who come from ordinary people. After forcing these people to give up almost everything they have, they always give the parents two days to think about what could happen, just to make them willing to do anything they ask to get their kids back safe. Then they send them back in body bags. Ray, Frank, I know this is a hellish thing for you to hear, but you deserve to know the reality of the situation. They must be stopped, and the time is now. People are going to get hurt bad and possibly end up dead in this battle. I don't have time to babysit anyone, so if you're in, I can't guarantee your safety. I can only guarantee you that they will know they've been in a fight, and I'll do everything in my power to stop these animals."

"How are we going to stop these monsters all by ourselves? It's like a suicide mission," Frank said.

"Hurricane and I faced bigger odds in the service, but I have to admit, Sam, we were much younger then. Hopefully, our experience will over-compensate for our age, my friend," Raymond stated. "I'm in, let's do it."

"Count me in also," Frank said, and then added, "This is my daughter we are talking about. If I lost her without trying everything possible, I'd never be able to live with myself. What are we going to do next?" he asked.

"Sam, as long as I'm here, I can also lend a hand," Jason Connors offered.

Sam nodded his head yes, then introduced the other two men. "Jason Connors, on the right, this is Frank Watkins. He's the father of Susan, one of the kidnapped girls. The man in front of you is Raymond Dupree, the father of Shirley, the other missing girl."

Jason shook both of their hands and said, "Aren't you the Sergeant who was wounded in Vietnam, which ended his chance to make Colonel?" Raymond nodded as Jason went on. "Both you gentlemen relax. If there is anyone capable of getting your girls out alive, it's this man here, and now with me it makes him even more dangerous. We will not fail."

"No matter what happens from here on, please don't question me on what I do. There is no room for mercy. If you can't stomach the violence I'll have to use, get out now. We only have one day left before they try and contact you. It's important we find out as much as possible before they make contact." Sam said, then added, "Those guys know a lot more than what they are telling us. At least one of them knows, and I promise you I'll find out who it is shortly."

With that said, they all returned back to the five men tied up. Steve started to talk first. "Hey, was I right about what that guy looked like? Can I go now? I promise I won't tell anyone what happened here and that you guys are onto them."

Sam spoke up, "I'm a man of my word. I said I'd let you go after you told me what I want to know. Unfortunately, I think one of you is holding out on me. So one by one, either you will tell me what you know, or die. Gentlemen, the choice is yours. I think I'll start with the man tied to the wheel." Hurricane walked slowly over to the wheel, and, without any warning, he kicked one of the guy's elbows that was woven in between the wheel spokes. There was a loud crack, and he screamed in a terrified voice as his elbow was completely dislocated from his arm. It just hung there like a rag. He had no control of his hand at all.

Frank almost felt sorry for the guy, but he also knew that someone knew where his daughter was. Right now, his mind was thinking about what his daughter must be going through with those other guys.

Hurricane stood there for a few minutes. When he knew he almost had the pain out of his mind, he brought the heal of his right foot crashing down on the guy's shoulder. He screamed as his shoulder snapped and then lay still on his side.

"Boy, Hurricane's tearing you apart piece by piece. If you were smart, you would tell him what he wants to know. Unless you want to lose every limb on your body, ask yourself if it's really worth it," Raymond told him. Then he looked at the other captives and said, "I hope you boys are watching your guy over here. See how brave he is? By the way, this is nothing compared to what Hurricane has in store for you."

"We don't know nothing, mister. Don't you think we'd tell you by now if we did?"

"Sam, Sam, Sam! Why can't you be quiet like your buddy next to you? He hasn't said a word," Hurricane stated.

"That's because he's still in shock from that screwdriver you put in his leg before. He never could take pain, even as a kid," young Sam answered.

"If that's the case, then let's wake him up and see," Sam stated as he opened his coat and revealed his throwing knives. He threw three so fast you couldn't even see the knife, but the screams revealed they hit their target. Each shoulder was hit, along with the other knee. "Now, if you want to live, tell me where the girls are," Hurricane said calmly.

When he went unanswered, he threw three more knives. Once again, they struck young Sam in the shoulders and the knee.

"You might as well kill us. We don't know anything, mister," Sam said.

"If that is your wish." With that, Hurricane threw two more knives, hitting his captives in the head. Their heads slumped down. "Two down, three to go. Who will be the sole survivor?"

Hurricane looked toward the toothless guy hanging on ropes. "Hey, you must be stretching out real good. Looks like you grew a few inches, and your feet are actually touching the ground. You've had a while to rest up. Now, let's see if your memory has improved."

Fear filled the man's eyes as he watched Hurricane move closer. He knew no matter what he said or did that he might die. Instead of stopping by him, Hurricane walked over to his army chest and pulled out what looked like a rivet gun and a glue gun, which he plugged into the little generator he brought. After filling it up with gas, he pulled the cord and instant electricity. He plugged in the glue gun and then turned toward the hanging man.

"Before we get started, my friend, what is your name?" Hurricane asked.

"My name is Zach. Are you going to kill me? And what are those tools for?" he asked in a frightened state of mind.

"What question should I answer first?" Hurricane paused a moment, then continued. "Well, let me tell you, Zachy. If you answer my questions without delay and I believe you, you may just live through this day. Whether it pans out or not will determine if you live past today and maybe beyond. As far as these tools, say I don't believe what you tell me, I may have to rivet your tongue to your lower lip and glue your ears shut. May I say, however, that the choice is totally yours. Whatever you choose, I'll make sure you get my full attention."

Zach was beside himself. He already had several teeth missing that he'd never get back. Would this maniac really do what he said? He's already killed Sam and Bobby. What is one more to him? Without his ears and mouth, he would certainly die a slow but certain death. Now he knew why he was called the Hurricane. He destroys anything and everything in his path, and he doesn't care how it gets done. "Alright, I'll take my chances and tell you what I know, but I want a guarantee that if it pans out

I go free."

"I can only guarantee you this, that if it doesn't pan out, you will wish that I had killed you fast. As for letting you go, we will first have to see where you take us," Sam answered.

Steve started threatening Zach, but Sam walked over to Steve and placed the rivet pistol on Steve's left hand that was taped tight to the chair, palm up. Without warning, Hurricane put a rivet right through Steve's hand and stuck it to the chair. Steve froze like he was in shock, then he started to scream.

"Now are you going to be a good boy and let this gentleman speak? Or, will I have to fasten your other hand to the chair as well?" Sam asked.

Steve shook his head that he was going to be quiet. He was in too much pain to talk. He was trying to block the pain out of his mind. It may have been easier if he could have moved his hand, but all he could do was watch as blood ran from his hand to the floor.

Meanwhile, Zach was explaining to Hurricane that they had no idea what they were supposed to do until Steve tells them. They had given them two choices in joining in. It was either help us, or we kill you—leave no witnesses or anybody else who can identify them, as they put it.

Even in his pain, Steve noticed that Hurricane kept watching him. His captor's eyes were like daggers piercing into him. He also had a feeling that no matter what happened, he was a dead man. Then Zach said something that Hurricane had not anticipated. "Every now and then, Steve has to call and check in with them, and he reports to them how things are going."

Hurricane walked back over to Steve. "You seem to be the contact man! Now, just how do you contact your friends?"

When Steve didn't answer him, Hurricane took out his knife and cut his pants around his pockets. When he didn't find anything, he picked up his jacket and started cutting his jacket to shreds. Finally, a notebook fell out of his coat. When Sam opened it up, there were five phone numbers on it. Steve knew what was coming before Sam spoke. He knew his number was coming up real fast, or could he make a deal with this maniac, he wondered.

"Steve!" Hurricane yelled. "Whose phone numbers are these? I'll find out sooner or later, so if you value what's left of your life, you'll tell me."

Steve knew he meant business, so he answered, "The top three are girls

I know, and the other two might happen to be the people you're looking for. I don't know who they are. I was sent an envelope with money and a note telling me to contact them every night at nine o'clock to report what was going on."

"When was the last time you called them?" Sam asked sternly.

"I called him last night. I was supposed to report tonight, but I guess I'm going to be late, aren't I?" Steve knew that was a mistake as Sam grabbed him and the chair and swung him around facing the window. Not saying a word, he then swung him around toward the open hay loft door. Then he pulled out what looked like a two-way radio, pulled up an antenna, and walked over to Steve.

"If you want to be able to see this sight tomorrow, you better make your call now, so we can trace the location. You have to keep him talking for at least three minutes."

"Why should I help you? Look at how you've destroyed me already. I've lost two toes, I have a broken leg, my left hand is no good to me anymore, and my tongue and lip are torn up. Now you want me to help you? Name me three reasons I should," Steve demanded.

"I'll give you one good reason," Sam started, "You see, I'm going to leave you tied up here until I find those girls, and if they should be harmed in any way while I'm wasting time with you, I'll come back and put you through so much hell, you'll beg me to kill you. But you'd better ask yourself this: will I be so merciful to you."

"Then if I help you, you'll let me go?" Steve asked.

"Let's just say that if I find them alive, there is a good chance of you being set free," Sam answered back.

"Give me that phone then!" he said.

After several rings, a voice came on the other end. "You're late! Why are you late tonight? Are there problems?"

"No! No problems, sir. I just lost track of time. Besides, I'm only five minutes late, so what's the big deal?" Steve asked.

"Five minutes could get someone killed, and we wouldn't want that to happen, not yet at least. We have to get the money first. Anything going on we should know about?"

Steve knew Hurricane was listening, so he was careful what he said, "No, everything is alright on this end. It's as quiet as a church mouse. Should

I call you back tomorrow at the same time as planned, sir?" Steve asked.

"Yes, just as we planned, and be on time tomorrow. It'll be a matter of life and death if you're late."

"Understood, sir. I'll call you tomorrow as planned," Steve said and hung up the phone.

"How did we do, Raymond?" Sam asked.

"I have a possible destination, but nothing definite. Another thirty seconds more and I may have had it. I think they had an untraceable line, however," Raymond answered. He paused and asked, "Then we are still half blind. I don't even know if what I have is accurate," Raymond finished.

"Raymond, you and Frank go and check on this possible place. Don't get cute. Just stay back, and if you see anything, call me back here." He handed each of them a radio of their own. "I'm going to try a couple of things on my computer. Hopefully, it can find what we can't, and if I get lucky, I may just find them. I still have a few tricks up my sleeve," Sam finished.

After Raymond and Frank exited the barn, Sam began his search.

Chapter Seven

While Sam, Raymond, and Frank were busy trying to figure out where the girls were, Susan Watkins and Shirley Dupree were going through their own torment. They had been taken to one of the upstairs bedrooms and locked in. The door knobs had been removed, and a skeleton key was the only way to unlock the door. With the windows boarded up, the girls had no way of getting out of the room.

Every time one of the captors would enter the bedroom, it was only to feed them. They either had on a mask or had the girls put a hood over their heads before they would deliver their food. Every now and then, one would cough or mumble something, but they would never come out and talk to either of them. Because of those darn masks they couldn't tell if they were the same guys who abducted them. Even their hair was covered, so they had no idea who was in the room with them.

It seemed like a lifetime had passed for the girls, even though it had only been a few hours. It must have been around seven o'clock when the door opened once again and food was brought in on trays. They were only given plastic eating utensils.

Shirley was thinking back to what her dad had told her. That seemed like so long ago now. He said that no matter how foolproof something looks, sooner or later somebody always slips up.

Then she remembered the screwdriver they found in the basement. It was inside of the boot she was wearing.

Susan and Shirley were trapped inside this boarded-up house. The two nightlights in the room gave off an eerie feeling, like being in the basement.

Shirley kept insisting that she had been here before. She closed her eyes and tried to envision the room she was in. Slowly a figure started to come clear in her mind. "This was my bedroom when I was young, and my brother Jimmy was in the room next to me. I was very young then. Jimmy was a little older, but it seems so clear. This was my bedroom. We lived here when I started to school. I remember a lot of screaming and things being broken. My father entered the house drunk and was beating my mother. When I opened my bedroom door, I saw my brother trying to help Mother. My father threw him down hard and broke his arm. Then from the shadow on the wall, I saw my father's arm come down and strike my mother. She fell down the stairs. Somehow, she crawled to the phone and called the police."

"I'm sorry, Shirley, I never knew."

"When the police arrived, my father was passed out on the bed. My mother was in my room crying. They arrested my father for assault and battery and for child abuse. I remember asking my mother why she always wore sunglasses when we went somewhere. She always told me the sun hurt her eyes."

Shirley was crying as her memories were slowly coming back to her. "This was my bedroom. Why am I back here? I've been a good girl. Is Daddy coming to beat me? Where's Jimmy?"

Susan grabbed hold of Shirley and tried to calm her down. "What are you talking about, Shirley? You're starting to scare me now."

"This was my house. Is my brother here?"

"What brother are you talking about? I thought you were an only child. Sorry, Shirley, I never knew."

"It's been so many years since I was in this room. I swore I'd never step inside this house again. Why am I here now?" Shirley asked.

"Do you think one of these men could be your father?" Susan asked without an answer.

"My father isn't supposed to be out of jail yet. He was convicted of some other things, too. I doubt that it was him," Shirley answered.

"Do you remember what the name of your street was, or maybe your address?"

"No, but there was a water tower close by. I could see it from here,"

Shirley answered.

Shirley and Susan were sitting on the floor eating, when they clearly heard some voices coming through the floor. They pulled back the carpet that was on the floor, and, bingo, there was a floor vent leading down toward the front room.

"I remember this vent. We used it to send heat upstairs. This room never had carpeting in it. That's why I couldn't remember it before," Shirley explained.

Susan gestured to Shirley to be quiet while they listened to what was being said in the room below, hoping maybe they could find out something. Instead, what they heard gave them chills.

"Hey, Chuck! After we get the money, do we take off right away and leave the girls here?"

"No, Glen. First, we'll come back and play with them a little. Then we'll send them home in body bags," Chuck answered.

Unaware that the girls were listening to them, one of the other guys spoke up, "Why do we have to kill them? They never saw our faces. They can't hurt us."

"Jerry, listen," Chuck said, "the reason we have never been caught is because we leave no witnesses."

"I realize that, but the other six girls saw our faces. These girls have done everything we've asked of them. They don't know who we are," Jerry suggested.

"I appreciate your input, Jerry, but we stick to our game plan. Nothing changes," Chuck said.

"These girls are only sixteen or seventeen years old at best. They are just kids. Why can't we just let them go?" Glen added in his two cents.

"If this upsets you two so much, we can always arrange for you to join them," Chuck answered.

"It's not that, Chuck," Jerry said. "It doesn't seem right, that's all I'm saying."

"Such is life," Chuck said, then added, "No more discussion about this. Let's go get ready to deliver our final ultimatum before we cash in. My friends, by this time tomorrow, we'll be leaving this fine State of Wisconsin richer than when we came in."

When the girls finally heard the front door close and the lock being applied, Susan asked Shirley for the screwdriver. They removed the screws holding the vent and took it out of the floor, they stuck the screwdriver threw the carpet that covered the hole.

Susan went to the door and used the screwdriver to try to get the latch on the door to release. When she had no luck, she decided to try and squeeze through the vent in the floor. After making sure the coast was clear, she very carefully squeezed her body through the vent hole in the floor. Because of her long lean body, she had no trouble fitting through. And because of her height, she didn't have too much trouble dropping to the floor.

She ran back upstairs and found the skeleton key and the door handle laying on the floor. After letting Shirley out, they ran down the stairs.

Susan went to the front door and used the screwdriver to try to pry it open. Then it dawned on her that they locked the door on the outside. She let out a shriek and tried to push the door open. Susan was just about to give up when Shirley said, "Susan, look, there is a stream of sunlight coming through the boards on that window, and something in the cushions of that couch is reflecting it."

"With the way our luck is going, it's probably just a pen," Susan said sarcastically.

Shirley walked over to check it out. She reached down between the cushion and the arm of the couch. "Susan, I think our luck has just changed."

Not wanting to appear too eager, Susan waited. Shirley pulled out a small pistol. At first, she thought it was just a lighter until she pulled the clip out.

"We have a gun! Not a big one, but it is still a gun. And it's loaded!"

Shirley pushed down farther into the couch and pulled out a big switchblade and a little penlight flashlight.

Susan came over and looked at the gun. She pulled out one of the bullets, and Shirley saw the look of disgust on her face.

"This is just a .22 caliber pistol."

"Yes. It isn't very big, but it can cause a lot of damage if you hit the right spot. That switchblade is at least four inches long. We finally have a chance of getting out of here."

"Shirley, you can't mean to kill them. I can't. I just can't do it!"

Shirley reminded Susan of what they had just heard. "You heard what they said. No matter if they get the money or not, they plan on killing us.

We only have this one chance. We need to make a plan of attack."

"Car doors, they're back."

"Quick, let's get back up to our room!"

As quick as two cats playing chase, they were back upstairs before the door opened. Susan placed the handle and key on the floor where she had found them and cautiously closed the door. Now they had to relax and slow their breathing, so their captors wouldn't get suspicious, or find out they had been out of the room. The door handle was inserted and in came a guy standing about five feet ten. He set down two plates of food and two sodas.

They thanked him, and he shook his head as a welcome and backed out the door. The girls went back over to the hole in the floor, so they could listen to the conversation downstairs.

"Well, gentlemen," one of them started, "by tomorrow night, we will be leaving Wisconsin and heading south to Tennessee."

"Why are we headed back down to Tennessee, Chuck?" another guy asked. "We just came through there from Florida. Why keep going back and forth?"

"If we keep moving up and down and side to side, it'll be harder to track us, my friends. Besides, we never leave a clear pattern to show where we might strike next," Chuck answered.

"That's why you are the leader, boss," a different voice spoke.

"Why, thank you, Glen," Chuck said. "Where is our messenger boy? And why hasn't he come back yet?"

"He said he had some unfinished business to take care of. He said he'd be back in a couple of hours, if not sooner," Glen answered.

"We don't really need him for this anyway. All right, boys, here is our plan of escape," Chuck said. "Glen, you and our invisible friend will stay back here. When we get the money, we will call you. After you kill our visitors, meet us back at the abandoned schoolhouse on the corner of Four Mile Road and Highway 38. There will be two different vehicles there. We will split up and keep in touch using our radios, just in case we run into some unforeseen mishap. If either of us ends up being tailed, the other car will back us up. Remember our motto: *We fight to the end, no surrendering!* Glen, you and your friend can do as you please with our guests—until the time comes to finish them, that is—so have fun. Now let's get some sleep. We have a very long day planned ahead of us. Glen, you enlighten Mr.

Invisible about our plans when he gets in. Jerry, Carl, and I will be in the next room. Just make sure you get plenty of sleep."

Shirley and Susan were petrified. No matter what they did or thought, there was only one way out—kill them, or end up dead. They had no other choice now. If they wanted to stay alive, they would have to kill.

Shirley started to pray, "Lord, I don't know why we were chosen to go through this, but if this is where our destiny ends, then I hope what I have to do to try to stay alive will not tarnish my hopes of joining You when my time comes."

"And I hope the Lord gives us the strength to fight back when the time comes and defend ourselves against these bastards," Susan added.

"Now, let's set up our own trap, shall we?" Susan stated.

Shirley nodded her head in agreement and, without saying a word, motioned for Susan to pass over the switchblade they found earlier. When she tossed her the knife, Shirley started to cut the carpet over the open hole in the floor. Susan just smiled.

"Without much light in the room," she whispered to Shirley, "that hole will be hard to see. Maybe we can get one of the boys to walk over that way and get stuck."

There was a small bed over in one of the far dark corners. They slid the bed over, and now it was totally dark. Then they gave each other the high five slap. Next, Susan took the knife and cut off a big piece of wood from one of the boards that closed off the window. She then inserted it into the knob hole, hoping it would prevent the men from getting into the room.

With only a limited number of items to use, there wasn't much they could do. They were just about to give up when Susan remembered the closet. Tiptoeing to the closet, they found two wooden closet rods, each about four feet long, but they were fastened to the walls. Without any light in the closet, Susan had to feel around to find whether screws or nails were holding the wooden rods. Just then, Shirley handed her the penlight she had found, and Susan saw that screws had been used. The screwdriver they had was too big, so Susan used the point of the switchblade to extract the screws. While Susan worked on the closet rods, Shirley was using the screwdriver to free up some floor board molding strips from the closet. Once Susan had freed the closet rods, she chiseled the ends into sharp points they could use for spears.

55

When they were finally done with what they hoped would work, Susan turned to Shirley and asked, "Shirley, you said before that you had a brother. I don't mean to be nosy, but what happened to him?"

"My mother told me that my father beat Jimmy so badly that they were afraid if he was ever released from prison he might go after him again, especially after he testified against him. So my mother granted them permission to place him in a foster home. I haven't seen him since, and I don't think I'd even recognize him now," Shirley answered.

"Why were they more afraid for him than for you and your mom?"

"When my brother testified against my father, he was given a much longer sentence than he thought he would get. As he was being taken out of the courtroom, he yelled at Jimmy, 'If I ever get out of here, I'll get even with you, boy.' The judge added two more years for his threat, but they also feared he might try to carry out his threat. Apparently, he had connections that might have helped him. Mother agreed, for Jimmy's safety, that he should be given a chance to live without fear, so she gave him up to another family who couldn't have children of their own. It was so hard for me to see him go, let alone for my mother," Shirley replied.

"I'm so sorry for your loss. And now you are going through this. Life is so unfair at times," Susan said, "but we are going to get out of this mess, I promise."

"Don't make promises you can't keep, Susan."

"This is one promise that I plan to keep. If we work together, I know we can make it out of here. After all, faith can move mountains, and we have the upper hand there. They won't be expecting us to be ready with weapons of our own. As long as we do things like we have planned, and nobody panics, we will survive," Susan said.

Shirley smiled and said, "I think we'll come out of this all right."

"Let's get some sleep. We can hear them coming. We have a long day ahead of us tomorrow, and we need to be rested up so we can give it our best effort."

Chapter Eight

What seemed like forever only took about fifteen minutes. The computer started spitting out information. "Bingo!" Sam yelled. "I think I finally have a location where the phone call took place." Sam called Raymond and Frank, "Hey, guys, where are you now?"

"We just passed a golf course on Highway 38 heading north," Frank replied.

"Great! At least we're in the same area. Keep following Highway 38 toward Six Mile Road. Turn left about three miles west. There should be a corner bar on Nicholson and Six Mile Road. The call was taken there," Sam instructed.

"Give us a few minutes, and we'll get right back to you. I just hope this is it," Frank said.

Sam's phone started to ring. "That was fast," he said, but when he answered it, he found a frantic Connie on the other end.

"Sam! Sam! We received another letter from the kidnappers!"

"Please, Connie, for all our sakes, take a deep breath, relax, and settle down. What does the note say, exactly?" Sam asked.

"They want one million dollars for each girl. They want it in small denominations, no larger than twenty dollar bills. We must have it by the time they call tomorrow at ten in the morning, or the girls will be killed. Sam, we don't have that kind of money. What are we going to do? I can't lose my daughter like this. I just can't!"

Sam interrupted her ranting and said, "Connie, hang up the phone now, and we'll be there shortly." Time was definitely working against them now. No more room for error. He just hoped Frank and Raymond would come back with some good news. Sam retrieved some duct tape and three little rubber balls from his truck. He walked over to the three living abductors left. One by one, he stuck a ball into their mouths and used the duct tape to make sure it stayed in place.

Then Sam turned to Jason and said, "We have a change of plans, man. Connie received another ransom letter. She's hysterical with the demands, and I can't say I blame her."

Just before he arrived at Raymond's house, Sam received a call from Frank. By the look on Sam's face, Jason knew it wasn't good. Sam realized it was almost eight o'clock. He instructed them to stay where they were and watch to see who answered the phone at precisely nine o'clock. Then Hurricane and Jason entered the house. Sam took the letter and asked if he could use a private phone to make a few calls. Connie led him into the den off the front porch. Within thirty minutes, Sam exited the room and said, "Ladies, and Jason, we need help. I have contacted the Sheriff's Departments and Rangers in the last ten states these hoodlums were in. They are sending in a few men to help our cause. They should be here in a few hours," Sam informed them.

"Sounds like they want them just as badly as we do," Jason replied.

Connie said worriedly, "But the note said …"

Sam walked over to Connie and said, "Connie, I know you were told if any police were called, they would kill the girls. But listen to what I was just told. The other ten families were told the same thing, and they did exactly as they were told to do. Their kids were sent home in body bags. Nobody ever saw their kids alive as they had promised. I'm afraid the same thing is going to happen here," Hurricane said.

The room suddenly went silent, and the two mothers started to cry. Sam knew he had to pull everybody together. It wasn't going to be easy, but as far as he knew the girls were still alive.

"What about the ransom money, Sam? There is no way we can raise that much cash," Anne told him.

"We set up a trap and hope it works. We lay low at the drop site, and when they pick up the cash, we follow them and hope they lead us to the girls," Sam said. "Until then, ladies, when they call, you call us, and we'll be here like a bolt of lightening."

"Where are you going now?" Connie asked.

"In twenty minutes, we hope to have a few answers."

Hurricane and Jason ran toward the truck. Jason asked, "Where to, partner?"

"Steve has one more call to make, and maybe, just maybe, we get lucky and nab one of them. Hopefully, Frank and Raymond are in the right place, and things will finally go right for us," Sam said.

It was ten minutes to nine when Sam pulled into the barn. They returned to the three abductors, still tied up and gagged. He wasn't playing games anymore. He was dead serious. The abductors couldn't miss Sam's eyes and the bolt cutter he was carrying.

"Gentlemen, time is running out for all of us. I am going to ask all of you one time, and only one time. First, Steve, you have to make a phone call, and you'd better be good, or I'll kill you where you sit," Hurricane warned.

At exactly eight fifty-nine, the number was dialed, and by the fifth ring it was answered.

"Hey, you're right on time tonight. Good boy. However, you don't have to call this number anymore. We've … What the … Who the hell are you?" Then there was silence.

Just as Hurricane was hoping, his phone rang. When he answered it, he received the news he was hoping for. "Hey, Sam, I hope this is the right guy, or we may be in trouble. The bartender was calling the police as we were leaving," Frank said.

"I'm sure he's our guy. I was on the other end of the line when it went down. Just don't drive too frantically, and get back here fast. Time is running out for all of us," Sam informed him and ended the call.

"Steve, now that you gave up one of the bad guys, I'm going to ask one question, and if I don't receive the answer I'm looking for, I start busting off body parts. I have the biggest oak bat that they make, and, yes, it will break off your wrists and ankles. Gentlemen, now that I have your undivided attention, 'Where Are the Girls?'" Sam yelled in frustration.

Hurricane walked over to the man twisted in the wagon wheel by his wrists and shoulders. "Maybe you, my friend, will enlighten me on where the girls may be."

He spat toward Hurricane. Observing the fire lighting up in Hurricane's eyes, he knew he had just made a deadly mistake. With his wrists and arms tangled through the wheel spokes, he was an easy target for what was to come. Sam raised his bat and brought it straight down on his left wrist. By the way it swayed in the air, they could tell in was busted clean off the bone. He kept on swearing in pain at Hurricane until his other wrist was hanging from his other arm. "All you have to do is give me an address, and all this will stop. Is that so difficult?" When Hurricane still had no response, he brought the bat straight up under his chin. He hit him so hard his neck sounded like a firecracker as it cracked, and his eyes rolled back in his head.

"I'm getting tired of these games, boys," Sam said. "If I have to kill all of you, so be it. I'll be doing the police force and the citizens of this great state a favor."

"There's no way you can get away with this. We have rights you know. This is illegal," the man hanging by his wrists said.

"So is kidnapping! I want answers, and I want them now. Jason, Frank, Raymond, I'm about to do something you might not approve of. If you can't handle it, please leave until I'm through." Hurricane walked over to his army chest once again, then turned and walked back with an evil grin on his face. Sam's arms tensed up as he began to walk toward that hanging man. In his massive arms he held a big bolt cutter. He lifted it toward the hanging man's feet. Without warning, he cut off his three little toes on his left foot.

"You crazy bastard, they took them to an old abandoned house. Please, just don't cut me again," he cried from the pain as he tried to keep his balance on the rest of his toes.

"I need an address!" Sam bellowed.

"I don't know the address. It was dark and had no street lights out there," he pleaded.

"Well, if you don't have an address, then you are no good to me," Sam said and then cut off his three little toes on his right foot. "Looks like if I cut off your ankles, partner, your arms may pull right out of your body," Sam said and then added, "Are you a betting man, my friend? If my calculations are right, I have three more cuts before you fall apart. Unless you have something to tell me that could help, let's see if you are willing to bet your life on it."

Sam knew he was getting close to finding out something, but this was still taking too long. He had to find some way to speed things up. He raised the bolt cutters, so he could see the blood on the blade. Then he lowered it slowly. Just as he started to cut and blood started to run down his ankle, he cried out.

"It was on the corner, it was the only house on the corner. Everything else was either a swamp or a very deep ditch. It was located on the North West corner. Honest, mister, that's all I know, but Steve knows where it's at," he cried.

Sam released the bolt cutters from his ankle and looked over at Steve. "You were willing to let all these men die, just to save your own hide?"

"Hey, can you cut me down now? I told you everything I know."

"Just hang around a little while longer until I find out if you're lying to me. Please don't interrupt me again," Sam snapped back.

"Steve, Steve, why don't you save us a lot of time and trouble and just give me the address? I'll relieve you of all your pain," Sam said.

"Are you kidding? They will kill me," Steve said.

Sam snickered, "Stevie, now that I know you are the main man here, with the answers, what makes you so sure I'm not the one who will kill you?" he asked.

"Because I have what you want, and if you kill me, you'll never see those tramps again," Steve hissed.

Steve would soon know he had said the wrong thing, as Hurricane raised the bolt cutters and cut off his left ear. Steve screamed in pain. Hurricane then proceeded to go around to his right ear. Steve started to sweat. When the sweat traveled to his cut-off ear, he let off a scream as the salt from his own sweat caused him even more pain. When Sam saw how much more pain he was in due to his own sweat, he cut the right nostril on his nose. He screamed from the sweat more than the actual cut. Sam couldn't believe how stubborn Steve was. He finally said, "Steve, sooner or later, you'll tell me what I want to know. So while you still have part of your face left, give me an address, and it'll be all over."

"You'll never get it, you crazy bastard. I'll take it to my grave. Those girls are just as dead as I am, so no matter what, I win," Steve said.

"You know what, Steve, I believe you, and since I'm wasting my time here, I should just kill you now." With that he pulled out his .357 Magnum and pointed it toward Steve's head. When Steve didn't even squint, Hurricane pulled the trigger. He untied him and let him fall to the ground.

With only one man left, Sam couldn't believe he had come up empty. This was the first time he couldn't squeeze out his answers. Suddenly his phone rang. He answered it, and it was Connie. "Sam, you're not going to believe this." After she told him what news she had, Sam answered, "Keep him there. I'll let the others know. We will all meet at your house."

When Hurricane hung up the phone, all he said was, "Well, my friend, I told you if I received the answer I wanted, I'd relieve you of your pain."

"Yes, you did, so am I free to go?" the hanging man asked.

"Yes, you can go as I promised. You can go straight to hell." Sam raised his gun and shot him in the head. Then he cut him down.

"Sam, we're not going to bury them?" Frank asked.

"No time, and besides, animals have to eat, too," Sam said as he started up his truck and headed back to Raymond's House.

Chapter Nine

S usan's alarm went off on her watch. She listened intently, to make sure nobody else woke up along with her. She nudged Shirley and couldn't believe that she could sleep through the noise from the alarm. Susan shook Shirley four or five times before she finally woke up. Shirley remembered where they were, as Susan said to her, "Wake up, sleepyhead. It's seven o'clock, and we have a little work to do before our guests arrive. If I heard them right last night, they plan on coming for us about ten thirty or eleven o'clock. We have to be ready to welcome them, so let's start getting rid of these lights in this room, shall we?"

They went around the room and pulled out all of the nightlights that were plugged into the outlets, except the one in their corner. They still had that penlight they found between the cushions of the couch last night. Then they quietly positioned the bed so it would hide the vent hole they had discovered in the floor.

Susan heard some commotion going on downstairs and wanted to find out what was going on. She motioned for Shirley to be quiet and listen. They both lowered their ears to the hole in the floor and listened intently.

"Hey, Glen! Where's Mr. Invisible?" one of the men asked angrily.

"I don't know, boss. He never showed up last night. Maybe something happened to him, or he got lost. This place is kind of hard to find at night. I guess that's why Mr. Big demanded that we use it. I never could figure out what was so special about this place that he would make such a big deal about bringing these girls here, other than it's already boarded up."

"Something happened to him alright. He came down with a case of cold feet. We'll deal with him later. It looks like you're on your own. Can you handle it?"

"There's two scared and helpless little girls upstairs. It's no problem, boss. After you call, they die. End of story."

"Good man. At least I can depend on you. But stop thinking so much. It's none of your business why Mr. Big wanted to use this place." The girls heard something like a slap on the back. "Just remember, if I don't call you by eleven thirty, something went wrong. You kill the girls no matter what and get out of here. Remember, when you're done here, you drive to the little schoolhouse on the corner of Four Mile Road and Highway 38. Drive careful and don't attract any attention on your way there. You'll have plenty of time. We're not planning on leaving this city until at least two o'clock when the coast is clear. Let's go and get this thing over with."

They heard several footsteps and the sound of the door closing. A car started up and drove away. The girls smiled at each other, "See, Susan, the odds are looking pretty good for us. This might be the break we were looking for. Now we only have to stop one guy named Glen," Shirley said.

They only had to deal with one guy, and they still had two hours to plan their strategy.

As they started setting things up, they heard some noise downstairs. Temptation was there, and they now tempted fate as they rolled back the carpet to see what was going on. Susan lowered her head slowly to check it out. She saw Glen tearing the couch apart as he muttered under his breath, "Where did I put that gun? I hope I didn't lose it. Even my knife is gone. Somebody is playing games with me. I hope I find it before I have to do my job."

Susan slowly pulled herself up from the hole with a smile on her face.

"What's so funny, Susan?" Shirley asked.

"I found out who those weapons in the couch belonged to," Susan answered, with a smirk on her face.

Shirley smiled back and said, "If these are his weapons, then he has no weapons. This keeps getting better and better for us."

"I wonder what he is going to use to kill us with then," Susan said sarcastically.

After removing the piece of wood from the bottom of the door and dislodging the piece of wood they had inserted in the handle, Shirley knocked on the door and yelled, "Hey! Could we get something to eat up here, please?" Then she whispered to Susan, "Let's have a little fun, shall we?"

Susan put a couple of the lights back into the wall as Glen delivered some food for them. Shirley tried to start up a conversation with him. "It seems awful quiet down there. Are you all by yourself?" she asked.

"The other guys are in the kitchen eating."

"What is your name, may I ask? You're kind of cute," Shirley told him, then added. "Maybe after this is over, what would you say about us going out to see a movie or something? What do you say to that?"

"My name is Glen, and that will not be possible after this is over."

"Why not, Glen? Are you going to kill us?" Shirley asked.

"This conversation is over. I have to go now, but I'll be back in a couple of hours and set you free," Glen said as he picked up the tray of dirty plates and exited the room.

"Well, talking to him about letting us go is out. We have no other choice than to kill him as he plans on doing to us," Susan said.

"Such a waste. He seems like a very nice guy," Shirley said.

"Just remember, that nice guy has orders to kill us in about ninety minutes," Susan said. "Shirley, you always had a way of liking the oddball guys, but half of the guys you dated were not half bad."

"Different strokes for different folks, my dear. I have always had a soft spot for the underdog," Shirley said laughing as she put the wood back in the tumbler and around the bottom of the door.

Chapter Ten

Since Frank and Raymond had his truck, Hurricane rode back with Jason. On the way, he phoned Frank and told him to meet them at Raymond's house. He wasn't exactly sure what was going on, but Connie had some good news for them. He told Frank to tie up that guy who had taken the call from Steve and put him in the back of his truck. He would deal with him later.

Jason and Raymond arrived at the house about the same time. Sam checked on the guy they had caught. He hit him hard in the jaw knocking him out cold. "That'll keep him quiet for a little while," he said and then proceeded to the house.

Connie and Anne were both sitting at the dining room table. Next to them was a young man who appeared to be eighteen to twenty years old. The three of them stood up as the four men entered the room. Connie started the introductions.

"Raymond, Frank, Sam, and I don't know you."

"Jason. My name is Jason. I'm a friend of Sam's, and it's a pleasure to meet you."

"I was just about to say," she continued, "that this is my son, Jimmy Wallace. Well, it *was* Wallace. It's now Simms. I had to give him up after my divorce because my ex threatened to kill him when he was released from jail. Now, after all these years, he's found me again."

Raymond shook his hand and said, "Son, I'm glad to finally meet you. Welcome to our home. I look forward to getting to know you, but right now, we have some important tasks to attend to. If you'll excuse us ..."

"That's why I'm here, sir, to help you!" Jimmy said.

"I appreciate that, son," Sam said, "but what possible help can you give us with this?"

"I know where they are keeping the girls, unless you already found out," Jimmy answered. "I didn't even know it was my sister until I saw my mother in the doorway when we dropped off the letter last night. I was watching from across the street when you opened the front door and pulled the letter off."

"Why are you even involved in the first place?" Raymond asked.

"Big mistake. They offered me five hundred dollars to help them. When I found out it included killing people and my own sister was one of the victims, I had a change of heart. I need the money, but I am not a murderer. I hope you have room for one more in your group. I'd like to see you nail these guys when I tell you where they are," Jimmy answered.

"Why should we believe you, Jimmy? How do we know this isn't a ploy just to take us farther from the meeting place?" Sam asked.

"No, sir, it's not, honest! This is my own sister we are talking about. I didn't think I had any other family still here in town. When I delivered that last letter and saw my mother's face, I knew I had made a big mistake, even if it wasn't my sister. I couldn't sit back and see someone get killed. Please, let me help you save my sister and her friend. I'll show you where they are, but we have to hurry. If we don't make it there by ten thirty, it might be too late," Jimmy pleaded.

Sam wanted to hear what Jimmy had to say, but before he could ask him, there was a knock on the front door. Sam opened the door, and his mouth fell open. There were at least thirty lawmen standing on the front lawn. Without turning, Sam spoke to those inside the house, "Hey, come look at this!"

When they had all walked out onto the front porch, one of the lawmen said, "Mr. and Mrs. Peterson, Mr. and Mrs. Watkins, I am Chester Mitchell of the Texas Rangers. We were very sorry to hear of what you and your families have been going through, and we hope we can help. It would be our honor to be included in the capturing of these outlaws. We all have good friends who have been victims of these madmen. Now we have a chance to finally stop them. I only hope that we will be able to extradite them to Texas when this is all over, for the simple fact that we have the death penalty and Wisconsin does not."

"We are more than willing to oblige any of you brave men and women in any way possible, Mr. Mitchell," Anne replied. "We don't care whether you capture them alive or dead. Just bring our daughters home safely ... please."

"Just call me Chester, ma'am. If we can't take them alive, we will make damn sure it's because they are dead and not because they've escaped! That's my promise to you and to all of those who have been hurt by them."

Sam stepped forward. "It's nice to meet you, Chester. I'm Sam Rufus. They also call me 'Hurricane.' I appreciate your promise, Chester, but let's get one thing straight right now. No matter what happens, these four guys must not walk away."

"What are you saying, Sam? We should go in for the kill no matter what?" Jason asked.

"Exactly! We can't let them go to court and risk walking on some kind of technicality. I've seen that happen too many times with these kinds of killers," Sam stated adamantly.

"Come to think about it ..." Chester paused as if in thought, "Sam, you're right. We can't take the chance of them ever being back on the streets again. I'm with you. Take no prisoners," Chester said.

"You won't have to worry about that," Jimmy said. "Chuck, the leader, has told everybody not to surrender, no matter what happens."

One of the other lawmen spoke up, "If that is true, then what are we waiting for? Let's go."

"Relax, guys. Let's get a game plan first. We can't go in there and not know what we are doing. For starters, Jimmy, tell us everything you know about their plans," Hurricane said.

"First of all, the girls are in a house on Seventy-Sixth Street off Highway U in Raymond. It's about a half mile down after the turn from Highway K. It's behind some trees, kind of secluded. I can ride with you and show you exactly. It's all boarded up, and I don't think anyone has lived in it for quite a while."

"I don't believe it!" Connie exclaimed. "That was our first house. Our kids were born there. The mailbox is on top of a wagon wheel. Right?"

Jimmy nodded yes to his mother and continued, "After the money drop,

Chuck will make the call to the house to kill the girls. Then we were supposed to meet them at an abandoned schoolhouse somewhere on Four Mile Road and Highway 38. His plan, I think, was to leave about two o'clock in the afternoon when the roads would not be as crowded."

"Sam, you're not going to believe this. We were only about ten minutes from the girls when we were at that barn," Raymond said.

"Well," Sam said, "we have a slight advantage now. Here is what we will do. Chester, you take these men with you and hide around that schoolhouse. When they enter the building, you will surround them and give them a big surprise when they try to exit. Jason, Raymond, Frank, and I will take Jimmy and go get the girls. Let's just hope we aren't too late. Do you have enough vehicles for this crowd, Chester?"

Chester told Sam they had left their vehicles parked along the street, and he thought they were good.

"Good. Let's synchronize our watches. It is now ten o'clock, time to fly, men, and good luck to all of you. If everything that young Jimmy here said turns out as planned, maybe the five of us will be able to join you in the fun at the schoolhouse."

About that time, the girls' friends, Jeff and John, walked up through the crowd of lawmen who were chatting among themselves. "I heard you may have found the girls," Jeff said to Sam. "John and I feel responsible. Is there anything we can do?"

"I think we're short one vehicle to bring the girls home," Sam stated.

About that time, John's father walked up to join John and Jeff. John introduced his father as Andy Anderson and told Sam that he had been with the Navy Seals. He and Sam exchanged knowing looks and shook hands. Andy asked, "Do you need any more help? I heard what's been going on, and I wondered if I could be of some assistance."

"Yes, you can my friend," Sam said. "How many cars do you have?"

"We have an SUV and a small car, and you're welcome to them."

"Well, Andy, we could use that SUV, and you as well. We all have our transportation now, but what we don't have is a car to bring the girls home and the delivery man. Would you be willing to take the money to the drop-off point?" Sam asked.

"I'll be more than happy to help in any way I can. Yes, I can take the money for you," Andy answered.

"Ordinarily, I would not ask someone to become involved without proper preparation, but in this case, we need someone who is a local and appears to be inexperienced to pull this off. You will have to pretend to be Frank Watkins delivering the ransom money for your daughter Susan and her friend. Can you do that, Andy?"

Andy assured Sam that he thought he could do it.

"If you don't mind, Andy, you can wait here for them to call with instructions on delivering the ransom. It should be very soon. The package is inside and ready to go. When this is over, I owe you a case of beer for being our silent partner," Sam replied.

"No need. Just bring the girls back home safe. That will be enough reward for me," Andy replied back.

"Alright, guys, let's give these bums a surprise party they'll never forget," Sam said. "Time is running short. I want to be ready for them before they have a chance to run. Frank, you follow us, but you can drive Andy's SUV, so we have a vehicle for the girls to ride home in."

They all let out a cheer and ran out to their cars. Like a flash, they were gone. Sam, Raymond, Jason, and Jimmy hopped into Hurricane's truck. Just as Raymond got settled in the front seat, he remembered and said, "Hey, Sam! We forgot about the guy in the back of the truck."

"No, I have something special planned for him," Sam replied. "Let's take him to our favorite spot in the barn."

Raymond nodded, "I think that would be a very good spot for him, Sam. He can finally see who his contact was. But we don't have time for any fun, so what's your plan?"

"We just tie him up for now and come back later. Let him sweat for a while, just like the girls are doing now," Sam answered.

"I like your thoughts. Let's give him something to really think about," Raymond said.

Sam nodded in agreement and headed toward the barn. Knowing it was only a few minutes away, he knew they had plenty of time before anything went down. When they arrived at the barn, he told the two in the back to stay put, while he and Raymond took care of their guest. When the back door was opened and their prisoner was taken out, Jimmy let out a cry, "Do you know who that is?"

"No, Jimmy, but we'll find out later," Sam said.

"I can tell you now. That is Louie, Chuck's brother. He's number two in this operation," Jimmy stated, his voice still raised in shock.

"He will not be doing any more kidnapping on this earth after we get done with him," Sam said. "This day keeps getting better and better," he added, chuckling as they led Louie into the barn.

Jimmy saw a shadow on the inside barn wall. It looked like a person being hoisted up in a chair. Shortly, he heard screaming, and Sam and Raymond came walking back to the car.

As they entered the vehicle, Jimmy asked, "What was he screaming about?"

"Sam just made sure he couldn't go anywhere if he were to break free," Raymond answered. "If he's still alive when we get back, we'll finish him."

Jimmy didn't ask any more questions. He was just very glad he had changed his mind about whose side he was on.

Chapter Eleven

It was almost ten fifteen when the phone rang. Connie answered the phone on the third ring. The voice on the other end was stern and muffled. "Is the person delivering the money there?"

"Yes, yes, he is. Can I talk to my daughter, please," Connie asked.

"All in good time. Now put the other person on, or I hang up and the girls die," the voice ordered.

Connie had tears in her eyes as she handed Andy the phone.

"Yes, I'm listening. Where do you want the money delivered?" Andy asked.

"First, what is your name?"

"My name is Frank Watkins. We have your money. Please don't hurt our girls," he pleaded.

"Do you have a bike?"

"Yes, I have a Harley," Andy answered.

"Not a motorcycle, a bicycle with peddles."

"I have a five-speed bike," Andy answered.

"Does it have a basket to carry the money in?"

"I can put one on it," Andy told him.

"Good. I want you to ride over to Lockwood Park. I'll call you on the pay phone. From there I'll give you more instructions on where to go next."

"Where is there a pay phone at the park?" Andy asked.

"You'll find it when it's ringing. By the way if you don't answer it by the sixth ring, the girls die. I'm giving you fifteen minutes to get there,

72

starting right now," he said and hung up.

Andy ran back to his garage and took down the bike. Both tires were flat. "Oh, great! Just what I needed," he said under his breath. Luckily, he had an air compressor nearby. He filled the tires and grabbed the basket to attach to the handlebars. He quickly placed the money bag in the basket and secured it with a bungee cord. He was off and riding. He looked at his watch. Only ten minutes to go.

"I'd better take the fastest route," he thought. He rode down to Haven Avenue and turned left. "This is a straight shot to the park. Ten blocks and I'm there."

A couple of blocks from the park, there was a traffic accident. He quickly took another left and rode up to Kinzie Avenue, then turned right. Just as he was entering the park, a phone started to ring, "Either my watch is slow, or they can't tell time," he mumbled to himself, peddling faster to get the phone. He counted the rings as he peddled faster and faster. Three rings … four rings … As the fifth ring started, Andy grabbed the phone.

"Hello, Sharon?" a male voice said.

"Sorry, son, but this is the park, not a girl's home," Andy replied.

"Sorry," the boy responded and hung up.

Andy couldn't believe how out of shape he really was. He was breathing heavily as the phone once again started ringing. After three rings, he answered.

"Very good," the voice on the other end said. "I'll have to make this next trip a little harder on you."

"Why are you doing this to me? Just tell me where to drop the money so we can get our children back," Andy pleaded.

"All in good time, Frank," he said. "I have to be sure you are not being followed. Now I want you to go to the Johnson Park Golf Course and wait for my call."

"Are you kidding me? That's at least a five- or six-mile ride. I'll never make it that far," Andy said.

"Well, if you don't make it there in twenty minutes, you can kiss your girls good-bye. However, just to show you I'm a fair man, I'll give you until ten rings. The clock starts now." Then he hung up.

Andy couldn't believe what he was doing. Suddenly, it dawned on him that maybe this is how they determine if the victims live or die. It must all be a sick game to these bastards. I hope I can see them get what's coming to them.

Andy was peddling like crazy. He was on Ohio Street heading toward Spring Street. Out of the blue, a car pulled up next to him. Andy was startled to see Victor Simons, another neighbor, slow down for him. Victor rolled the window down and shouted, "Where to?"

"Spring Street," Andy yelled back.

"Hang on to the window," Victor yelled.

Andy held on, and Victor drove him toward Spring Street. When they got to the corner, Andy noticed people stopping traffic and waiting for him to turn. "What's going on?" he wondered. "This is unbelievable. It's like everyone knows what I'm doing. But how?"

He held on to the window as Victor slowly turned the corner, being careful not to lose him and the bike.

"Where to now?" Victor yelled again.

"Johnson Park Golf Course," Andy replied, "but I'll drop off before we get there." Andy held on as Victor drove him up Spring Street toward Emmertsen Road, he was only about a mile and a half from the park, but at least two or three miles from the outside phone. He knew where this phone was because he played golf there often. He looked at his watch as Victor slowed to drop him off at Three Mile Road. They didn't want to risk him being spotted getting help.

Andy peddled toward the phone knowing he had at least six minutes before the call would come in. He relaxed as the light breeze calmed down his nerves. Just as he arrived at the public phone, it started to ring. Andy let it ring nine times before he answered to make it sound as if he was winded.

"See, Frank, you underestimated yourself. You must be in pretty good shape. You're almost done. Only one more run, and it's over. Now, I want you to ride to the Caledonia Mount Pleasant Park. Once again, you have twenty minutes to complete your ride. There is a red building as you enter the park. There is a green garbage can in front by the big doors. Take out the green bag that is inside the trash can, put the money inside, and walk away."

"Wait, what about the girls? Can I pick them up after dropping off the money?" Andy asked. "If I don't see the girls there, you get no money."

74

"Frank, I thought you loved your little girl and her friend, but if you are trying to play hardball, I'll piecemeal your lovely girls back to you. Now, are you ready to play by my rules?" he asked.

"Okay, you'll get your money, but when do we get our girls?" Andy asked.

"When you open the green bag, there will be an address in it. Your girls will be inside that house, locked in the bedroom upstairs. Don't even think about taking the money and running because, if I don't see the money, I make a call, and the people keeping your girls company will kill them. Do you understand me, Frank?" he asked.

"Yes, I understand, but could I have a little bit more time. That's another five- or six-mile ride, and I'm tired," Andy pleaded.

"Alright, Frank. I'll give you an extra five minutes. I'll call you in twenty-five minutes. If the money has not been delivered by then, you know what will happen."

Andy was exhausted when he exited Johnson Park. He was just about to turn left when Victor drove up next to him. "Where to now?" Victor yelled.

"Caledonia Mount Pleasant Park," Andy yelled back. Once again, Andy held on and was on his way. From out of nowhere a police car was behind Victor. When Victor pulled over, Andy had to keep going and flew right on by. When the police officer walked up to the car, he asked Victor to step out. "What's going on here?" he asked.

Victor clued him in on the situation. The officer told him to hold on. Victor watched as he walked back to his squad car. He opened the door and got in and made a call on his car radio. Shutting off the lights and the engine, he got out and walked back to Victor's car. "Come on," he said, jumping into the front passenger seat.

"What are you doing?" Victor asked.

"I want to help. I'm Officer Todd Kopecky. Is that some kind of problem?"

"Yes, your uniform. He said no police. If he sees the uniform, the girls are dead," Victor said.

"No problem," Officer Kopecky said, taking off his shirt. "My T-shirt should look normal."

"Thank you," Victor said as he drove off. They spotted Andy about a mile ahead of them.

When Victor drove up beside him, Andy thought he was seeing things. The police officer smiled at him and gave him a "let's go" nod. Once again, Andy grabbed the open window and breathed a sigh of relief as they picked up speed. "Another three miles, and we are home," he said to himself. "I just hope the others make it to the girls before this is over."

"Bingo," Andy said as he entered the front gate. Victor had dropped him off down the street, and he had almost eight minutes left. He walked over to the trash can, found the green bag, opened it, and just as the voice on the phone had said, there was a note inside an envelope. The instructions on the outside of the envelope said, "Not to be opened until instructions have been given."

When the phone rang, it startled Andy. He was concentrating on the envelope.

"Have you completed your task?" the voice asked.

"I just arrived and opened the bag. I'm putting the money into the trash can now," Andy said.

"Negative!" the voice said. "You will take it to the swings and give it to the janitor working there. He has instructions on what to do with it. And then you can go get your girls. This is the last time you will hear from me." With that, the connection ended.

Andy did as he was told. The janitor accepted the money and was off and running. Andy finally opened the envelope.

> *Did you really think it would be that easy?*
> *Those bitches are already dead. Ha*
> *Good luck finding them.*

Andy's shoulders slumped, and he said a prayer that the others made it to the vacant house in time.

Chapter Twelve

Shirley and Susan were trembling with fear. As time went by, they both knew what they had to do. The question was, could they really do it when it mattered. One thing was for sure. When this day was over, they would never be the same again. It would be hard deciding what to do as an adult, but to be seventeen and to have to decide on killing someone or be killed? That would take a long time to erase from anybody's mind. Hopefully, they would be the same fun-loving girls they were before this happened to them.

Susan removed the remaining nightlights, except for the one behind them. They wanted it so dark when he opened the door that he couldn't see. This would even the score for both parties. The alarm in Susan's wristwatch suddenly came on, startling both girls. They knew it would be show time soon. Shirley went over to the last nightlight and pulled it from the plug. Susan turned on the little flashlight so Shirley could see where she was. As soon as she was in place, it was shut off.

Susan glanced at her watch. It was ten forty five when they finally heard someone trying to insert the doorknob into the door.

"What the heck is going on?" he said as he bent down and looked into the tumbler. "Very smart thinking, ladies, but I'm afraid that will not keep me out very long." He inserted a screwdriver into the opening, and in a few minutes, the sliver of wood was punched out, and the door knob was inserted. He turned the knob and pushed. They heard his head hit the door. "You girls must think you're pretty cute, but all you're doing is making me mad. I don't have time to waste, so as soon as I get into this room, you're dead. I was going to have some fun with you, but I'll have no time for that now." He kicked the door and the bottom panel cracked. He broke the rest of the door panel, squatted down, and entered the room. "Those damn lights must have burned out. I can't see a thing. I wish I had my flashlight now. Where are you girls, anyway?" he asked.

"We are right over here by the bed, Glen," Shirley called out.

"No, we are over here by the bed," Susan called out from the other side of the room.

"How do you know my name? Where are you? It's so dark in here I can't see a thing," Glen said.

"We heard you talking downstairs earlier," Shirley said.

"There's no way. You couldn't have heard what we said," Glen said.

"Let's see, there is Chuck, Jerry, Carl, and you. Oh, and one or two mystery men we do not know," Susan said.

"Impossible! You're just guessing, trying to find out something from me … which will not matter after I get my hands on you two. Now, where are you?"

"Just follow the bed. You'll find us on the very end," Shirley said.

He followed the sound of her voice and found the bed. He walked slowly down the side and suddenly let out a scream as he found the hole in the floor. He hit the hole hard. The girls could tell he was in very bad pain.

Shirley inserted a few nightlights to see what had happened. She started laughing when she saw their enemy trapped in the hole. One leg was through the hole, and the other was straight out from his body. He must have hit so hard that he hurt his privates and knocked himself out. He did not move as the girls jabbed him.

They looked at each other and laughed. Susan said, "This was easier than I thought it would be."

Just as she was saying that, he reached out and grabbed her right ankle and started to pull. Shirley saw what he was trying to do and grabbed hold of Susan. A tug of war ensued. Shirley grabbed one of the clothes rods they took out of the closet. She ran over by Glen and slammed the end right down on his arm. He let go instantly and was in obvious pain. They could see the anger in his eyes. His voice was husky, "As soon as I get out of here, you two are dead."

Glen was trying to pull himself up out of the hole and did not see Shirley approach him. Suddenly, she stuck the sharpened end of the other pole into his good leg with unbelievable force for her size. "So what did you think, Glen, that we were just going to stay here and do nothing but wait for you to come in and kill us? You'd better think again because, right now, Susan and I have the upper hand, and we are going to make you pay for what you've done to us."

Glen looked up and, for the first time, saw the gun they were pointing at him.

"Where did you get that gun? That thing wouldn't hurt anyone, let alone kill them," he said.

"We found it where you left it, in the couch, and if it couldn't kill anyone, why were you in such a panic a couple of hours ago trying to find it?" Susan asked.

"You were locked up in here. How could you have found my gun?" Glen asked.

"You boys were not as thorough cleaning up as you thought. Susan and I found a screwdriver down in the basement. We managed to open up the door with the screwdriver and search the house. And look what else we found," she said. She pushed the button on the switchblade, and the long, four-inch blade appeared. "Is this what you were going to kill us with, Glen?" Shirley asked.

Glen turned almost as pale as a ghost as her voice changed to an angry tone. He knew he was trapped. His right leg was in the hole in the floor. His left leg was stretched out from his body. From the force and the awkward way he fell, he knew he had ruptured something. On top of that, the taller girl speared his left ankle, and blood was bubbling out of it. He was trapped, and he knew they had him at their mercy. The ball was definitely in their court. He was just hoping he could keep them talking long enough to climb out of the hole he was in. Slowly, he was moving toward getting out. He kept his bottom sliding slowly across the floor while he talked to the girls.

"Now, why would you think I would kill you?" he asked, trying to confuse them.

"We heard what you were told to do after you received your phone call. We were eavesdropping through that hole in the floor that you found,"

Susan said.

"I wasn't going to kill you. How could I kill two beautiful-looking girls like you?" Glen asked.

"Why did you say you were going to kill us before when you couldn't open the door?" Susan asked back.

"I was just mad at that moment. You pulled a good one on me. I didn't really mean I was going to *kill* you. It was just a figure of speech," Glen said sweetly, trying to win them over.

"Do you think we have 'Stupid' stamped on our heads, Glen," Shirley asked before she stomped on his hands with her heavy shoes.

"Why did you have to do that?" he asked.

"Why are you trying to crawl out of your hole? What will you do when you get out?" Shirley asked.

"I'm just trying to relieve some of this pain I'm in. Do you really think I'm in any physical shape to hurt you?" Glen asked.

"We will help you out of the hole if you promise not to try anything funny," Susan said.

"No!" Shirley screamed at Susan. "Let him get out by himself. Don't put yourself in a position that gives him any kind of upper hand."

"What are you, a cop or something?" Glen asked.

"My father is a cop and a damned good one. Looks like you picked on the wrong girls to harass this time. My father will find us, and you and all your friends will all go to jail," Shirley said.

"He'll never find us in time. Nobody has yet. He knew if he brought the police into this, we would kill you. We haven't seen anybody helping him in a blue uniform yet. Besides, we never make a mistake. That is why we've never been caught," Glen said.

"You've never made a mistake *until now*, you mean," Shirley said.

"What mistake?" Glen asked curiously.

"You gave my dad two days to do some research," Shirley answered.

"There's no way he can find us in two days," he said.

"You don't know how powerful my dad's friends are. I wouldn't be surprised if he showed up here any minute," Shirley said.

"You must have that 'Stupid' stamp on your head after all. There is no way he'd be able to find us," Glen replied.

"What time do you have to meet your friends, Glen? Time is running out for you, isn't it?" Shirley asked.

Just as she completed her question, he made a lunge toward them. He was hurting, but his adrenalin was keeping him from feeling anything. He grabbed the gun from Susan's hand and sat down on the bed, motioning for the girls to step in front of him. He looked at his watch. He had plenty of time left, so he thought he'd make these girls pay for what they had done.

Chapter Thirteen

Sam, Jason, Frank, Raymond, and Jimmy were on their way to the house where the girls were being held hostage. Sam, knowing he was running out of time, hit the road driving like he was in the Indianapolis 500 race. His speedometer indicated 75 miles an hour just as he passed under the I-94 intersection at 20 miles over the speed limit.

Suddenly, they had company. With lights flashing, a state trooper came up behind him like bees drawn to honey. Sam pulled over and said under his breath, "Great, just what we needed."

"May I see your license and registration, please?" the officer asked.

"Officer, we are in a hurry, and it is a matter of life and death," Sam told him.

"Can you step out of your vehicle, please?" Sam stepped out of his truck.

"Have you been drinking, sir?" he asked.

"No, Officer, I'm just in a bit of a hurry," Sam answered.

"It says here you're a P.I. Are you on a case, sir?"

"Yes, Officer, that is what I've been trying to tell you. Now, can we please go?" Sam asked.

"Well, Mr. Rufus, I really need to see some other form of identification. We've had a few car thefts in this area, and fake identification cards have been used," the officer said.

"I'm sorry to have to do this to you, Officer, but there are two girls who could end up dead if we don't get there on time," Hurricane told the officer, "and you keep wanting to play footsy after I've told you several times that this is a matter of life and death."

Realizing that this stop was going sour quickly, the officer took a step backward and unsnapped his holster. "Who are these girls you're talking about?" Before he had a chance to even finish asking his questions, Sam spun the officer around and had him handcuffed to his own squad car. Raising his voice, Sam instructed the officer, "Call headquarters and tell them we could use some more help. We'll be in Raymond off of Seventy-Sixth Street, a mile or two north of Highway K." Hurricane turned to leave and yelled back at him, "Tell them to hurry and send an ambulance."

Then he drove off like a rocket. He knew they had wasted too much time with that patrolman. He was only doing his job, but time was running out. Sam was driving at a high rate of speed wanting to make up time. Frank looked at the speedometer. Ninety-five miles an hour. Sam slowed to forty-five as he made his turn on Highway U. Jimmy felt like a piece of bologna being squished between two slices of bread in the back seat. Hurricane was driving extremely fast, and then Jimmy suddenly yelled out, "There it is! There's the turn!"

Sam slammed on the brakes. Good thing everyone had seat belts on, or the windshield may have been shattered. He backed up and turned into the driveway, hoping no one in the house would hear the truck coming. About three quarters of the way in, Sam shut off the motor. "We'll walk from here. Try to be quiet. Let's surprise whoever is inside. Let's make this fast and get back to the other marshals. Why should they have all the fun?" Sam said, then added. "All set?" Everyone nodded yes. "Let's go. Good luck, and watch out for the girls." They headed toward the door.

Inside the house, Glen started laughing. "Well, looks like the cavalry you girls were waiting for isn't going to make it, and the time has come for us to say our goodbyes." Glen got up from the bed, standing as straight as he could considering his condition.

The girls knew he wouldn't be able to move very fast, so they decided to go to plan B. Shirley clicked the switchblade open. As soon as Susan heard the click, she fell to the floor, acting like she had fainted.

When Glen looked away, Shirley threw the knife toward him. It was a perfect throw, right to his stomach. Glen looked completely surprised. He had forgotten about the knife. He couldn't believe she would actually throw it at him. It stuck him good, and he knew he was in trouble. He tried to raise the gun to shoot Shirley, but just as he was about to fire, Susan brought her foot up between his legs. The jolt and the sudden pain he felt caused him to pull the trigger, but it was a wild shot and missed Shirley completely. Glen fell to the floor, writhing in pain.

Within seconds of the sound of the shot, the front door burst open, and in came the cavalry. Sam ran up the stairs, peering through the door that was standing open. It took a moment for his eyes to adjust to the darkness. Then he saw Glen holding the gun. "Freeze," he yelled.

Glen wasn't listening as he raised his weapon. Sam fired. The bullet from his .357 Magnum hit Glen's right hand, almost tearing his hand completely off his wrist. Glen was in complete shock as he saw that cannon of Hurricane's. He knew this gig was up.

"Frank, Raymond, the girls are up here, and they are fine," Sam yelled out the door.

Within seconds, the girls heard the men running up the stairs, and then their fathers entered the room. A welcome sight they were! The girls ran to them, and after a few moments of hugs and kisses, Shirley turned to Glen.

"Glen, meet the cavalry—our fathers and their friends."

"How did you find us?" Glen asked.

Shirley's eyes finally saw someone who looked familiar to her. She walked over to him and slowly asked, "Jimmy, is that you?" When Jimmy smiled, she grabbed him and gave him the biggest bear hug ever. "I would know that smile anywhere, but what are you doing here?" She asked him.

"Ladies, meet the invisible man," Glen said.

Shirley looked confused, "Were you in on this whole thing?" Suddenly, she had a memory. "That was you in the van, wasn't it? I knew there was something familiar about you!"

"They told me no one would get hurt. Then I found out they planned all along to kill you girls. They sent me out to deliver the letter, but when I saw it was Mom, I couldn't go through with it. So I decided to end all of this and let them know everything I knew. And that's why we are here," Jimmy explained.

"You're a dead man when Chuck finds out, Jimmy," Glen said.

"Don't worry, Jimmy," Hurricane said. "After the little surprise party we planned for Chucky boy, I don't think he'll be around long enough to hurt anyone. Besides, if Chucky is anything like Glen here, maybe we should send you girls into that building. It's a good thing we showed up here when we did, or Glen would have been dead already. You underestimated your opponents, didn't you, my friend? You should never judge a book by its cover. Even a little mouse will stand and fight when backed into a corner."

"As long as you have no intention of letting me live, could you just answer me one question? Who are you guys?" Glen asked.

"Frank and Raymond are the fathers of these girls. Jimmy you already know, but you didn't do your homework very well because Jimmy happens to also be the long-lost brother of Shirley here. Jason is a fantastic expert with a sketch pad and a pencil, among other things. And I am known by one name—'the Hurricane,'" Sam answered, and then he shot Glen in the head.

Hurricane walked over to Glen and started searching his body. He found his car keys in his pants pocket and tossed them over to Jimmy. "Jimmy, you get the girls home safe. We still have some unfinished business to take care of."

"I'd rather go and help you guys. I feel responsible for all of this," Jimmy said back.

"Jimmy," Hurricane started, "you've already been a great help to us all. I'd feel better if you were not there for the simple fact that, if something should go wrong and he gets away, he will think you're dead and will not search for you. Besides, you have to get reacquainted with your real family, and the girls need to get back home. Please take them home, so at least we know all of you are safe," Hurricane finished.

Jimmy nodded his head with a gesture that said he understood. Then he looked at the girls with a bright smile and said, "Ladies, shall we go?"

When they were almost out the door, Hurricane yelled, "Hey, wait, ladies. Let Jimmy tell you how he saved your lives today. If not for him, we may not have found you in time. He's your knight in shining armor."

The girls were very interested in his story and were prying information out of him as they walked out to the car. Jimmy started up the car and drove slowly out of the driveway.

As soon as they heard the car drive off, Hurricane continued searching Glen. He found a two-way radio in his inside pocket. He took it out and turned it on. Within a few minutes, a voice came on the radio. "Glen, good buddy, are you there? Glen, answer the radio. Then they heard another voice, "Maybe he's still having fun with the girls, boss." They all laughed and another voice spoke up, "Maybe he's burying the bodies."

And then they heard, "Hey, Glen, this is Chuck. In case you have the Record turned on, we are headed for the schoolhouse now. It's on the corner of Highway 38 and Four Mile Road. When you get there, we will split up the cash and go our separate ways. Call me back if you're going to be longer than planned. Over and out."

"This may come in very handy," Hurricane stated. "Let's get going. We have no time to waste."

They all ran out to Sam's truck and jumped inside. "Ready for round two, boys?" he asked as they pulled away. They all nodded their heads, but deep down inside, both Frank and Raymond had butterflies in their stomachs. Neither of them knew if they could kill a man as easily as Hurricane had done. Raymond had gone through some pretty hair-raising times with Hurricane in the military, but during this skirmish, it had been Hurricane who had done all of the killing. They would soon have the opportunity to find out the answers to their questions.

Chapter Fourteen

Hurricane left the radio on as they drove toward the little schoolhouse. Everyone was silent during the trip until Raymond opened up and said, "I'd like to thank you guys for helping us get our daughters back safe. I've always said I am a very lucky man to have a family like I have now. I didn't realize how extra lucky I was to have friends like you three."

"Don't go and get mushy on us now, Raymond," Sam said and then added, "Besides, I would have been extremely upset if you had not called me, and I read it in the newspaper or saw it on the news."

"I have two children of my own, and I can only imagine what I'd be going through if that was my child. I'm more than glad to help out in any way I can," Jason added.

"When I think of what those girls must have gone through the past two days, I just want to break all their necks," Frank said.

"That's the attitude you will need when we get there. Just keep thinking what your daughters went through as you take aim at those guys," Hurricane said.

Just as Hurricane was about to turn onto Highway 38, he was surprised when voices suddenly came through the radio. "Hello, boss. This is Chuck. I've not heard from Louie or Glen, and I'm getting a little worried. I tried both of their radios, and nobody answered."

"Well, Chuck, my boy, you seem to be having problems controlling your men. Maybe I should find somebody else who can get the job done," a voice came back to him.

"No, that ain't it, boss. We've never had problems before. Maybe their radios are out of range. I'll try 'em again in a little while. Then again, they may just about be here. I'll wait a few more minutes and check on 'em again," Chuck replied, not wanting his boss to get upset.

About that time, a voice in the background yelled, "Hey, Chuck, check this out." In the commotion, Chuck forgot to turn his radio off. Hurricane and the others heard their conversation: "What the hell? We've only got five hundred dollars here. I'll get those bastards, so help me … Glen, if you can hear me, kill those girls now. That's an order."

"If you have any more problems, call me back," Chuck's boss announced with irritation in his voice.

"We've just received a big curve ball, guys," Hurricane stated.

"Yes, we caught that conversation. Now what do we do?" Jason asked.

"We have to get to that schoolhouse before they decide to kill everyone," Hurricane said and stepped on the gas.

"Why don't you just radio ahead, Sam?" Frank asked.

"I thought about that, Frank, but if these radios are on the same frequency as ours, they might hear what the plan is and try to get away. We need to try and take at least one of them alive," Sam answered.

The fifteen minute drive to Highway 38 took Hurricane five minutes at his 90 mph speed.

Jason was getting a bit nervous, not because of how fast Hurricane was driving, but because it was almost like he was a man possessed. He took the turns at a high rate of speed, and if the light was red, he drove right through it. When Sam turned onto Highway 38, and Jason saw the curves on this road, he had to do something. He figured he would try to ask Hurricane some questions, hoping it would bring him back to reality.

"Sam, this is a very unusual vehicle. Where did you come across such a truck? It reminds me of an altered military vehicle, almost like a bigger version of a Jeep."

"This *is* a very unusual vehicle, my friend," Sam stated. "You have a very good eye for detail. This was one of those Land Rovers used by the military. They are built for rugged terrain and for driving through muddy and sandy areas," Sam answered, not slowing his speed.

"How did you come to own one of these, Sam?" Jason asked curiously.

"Well, Jason, I had this buddy who worked in the graveyard. That's where they send the vehicles that are beyond repair. Just before I left the service, I inquired about possibly buying one of those trucks. I went through all the channels, from the supply sergeant all the way up to a four-star general. After a lot of explaining why I wanted one of these trucks and signing a lifetime contract that if I sold it to anyone else except back to the military I could end up in a military prison, I received permission. But it also cost me three cases of beer, two cases of Havana cigars, and a couple of my paychecks," Sam answered, slowing down to a normal rate of speed.

"Even though you paid for the truck, it cost you all those extras? That's not right," Jason said.

"Well, the truck I wanted had a blown engine in it, so that little extra was for having a new engine delivered to my house, courtesy of the United States Army. I altered a few areas in the truck and added a few hiding spots here and there, and this is my finished product," Sam finished.

"Well, it sure drives smooth. If it didn't have windows, you would never know you were moving," Frank added.

"I installed some very heavy suspension springs because of all the extra weight I carry," Sam replied.

They finally arrived at the schoolhouse. Sam drove a short distance past it and parked in a field. The four men ran back to join the posse already there. Sam instructed the men to split up, with each person going in a different direction. They would then regroup and tell what they had heard. They had to try to take at least one person alive. Sam brought the radio along in case something else came up.

They looked at their watches. It was almost two o'clock. Something was bound to happen soon. The boss's voice came back on the radio, "Have you left the school yet?"

They listened.

"We're still waiting for my brother and Glen," Chuck said.

"We go as scheduled. Glen and your brother know where you're going. They can always meet us there," the voice instructed.

"Yeah, I suppose you're right," Chuck answered. "We'll pack up and head out quick. We'll be picking you up in approximately fifteen to twenty minutes. Be ready," Chuck said.

"I'll be here with bells on. See you soon. Over and out."

As Sam turned around, he saw Jimmy coming up toward them, "What are you doing here? I thought I told you to take the girls home and stay there," Sam snapped at him.

"You told me to take them home, but you never said I had to stay with them. Besides, I heard that voice you heard on the radio, and it might have been my father," Jimmy said.

"How would you know that?" Raymond asked him. "You were very young when they put him in jail."

"Yes, but I'll always remember his voice. It was drilled into me. It was rugged, and he always sounded like he was drunk," Jimmy replied.

Sam sat down and listened as Jimmy told him what he remembered about his early childhood. He couldn't believe what he was hearing. "How could anyone treat their children and wife that way?" Sam thought to himself as the story was told.

"I thought he still had a couple of years left in prison. Do you think they let him out early?" Jimmy asked.

"I'm not sure, Jimmy. We will find out after this is over. I promise," Sam replied. "Right now, we have to end this reign of terror and find out who and where this mystery boss man is that's behind it."

Suddenly, the school doors opened and out stepped three of the scariest looking guys Sam had ever seen. They waited until all three were totally out of the building and then walked toward their vehicles. Just as they got there, one guy started to yell, "What the hell is this? I have a flat tire. Hey, Jerry, will you give me a hand changing this flat?" he asked.

"That's Carl," Jimmy whispered to Hurricane and the others with him.

"No, man, that's your problem," Jerry answered Carl. "Besides, it's too spooky out here. I want to get out of here as soon as possible."

"Too spooky? What's your problem, man? As peaceful as it is out here, what could possibly happen? Besides, it'll only take us maybe five minutes to change this thing, and then we'll be on our way," said Carl.

"Alright, I'll help you out, but just remember, you're going to owe me a big favor later," Jerry replied.

They opened the trunk and discovered there was no spare in the car. "Who in their right mind would drive around without a spare tire?" Carl hissed. He was angry!

"Looks like the man that used to own this car would," Jerry said with a sinister laugh.

Chuck finally said, "This isn't a big problem. You and Jerry ride together for awhile, and when we come to the first rest stop, we'll just borrow another car. Now, let's get going. Time is running out for us."

Just as they were about to get into their vehicles, Chester stood up and yelled from the brush across the street, "United States Marshals. You are surrounded. There is no escape. Turn around and put your hands on top of your car and stay still."

"Like hell we will," Chuck said, pulling two pistols out of his coat as he turned around and started firing.

When the three men started to run back to the building, the officers opened fire on them. Bullets were being sprayed all over the three men as they tried to hide behind the cars, but they soon learned that they were completely surrounded. Jerry and Carl were both hit in the legs as they tried to run. Sam couldn't understand why they didn't just give up. He'd rather take them alive at this point. He could always kill them later. Besides, this time he needed answers to a very important question.

Sam was thinking that if Chuck was hit, they might just give up. Looking through the scope on top of his rifle, Sam set his sights on Chuck's legs. He took his shot, and Chuck started screaming and rolling around on the ground. The bullet had penetrated right through both legs. Chuck was now helpless. He wasn't going anywhere. As soon as Chuck was hit, both Jerry and Carl raised their arms in the air and started yelling, "We give up! Don't shoot!" Chuck was in no position to argue, at this point.

The posse moved into sight for the first time, you should have seen the eyes on the three men lying on the ground bleeding. Thirty-six sheriff's deputies, marshals, and some of Caledonia's finest came out from the brush and crossed the street.

Chapter Fifteen

H ey, Chucky, it seems like you just might be the man I was looking for. By the way, your brother sends his love, and he's sorry he couldn't be here with you," Hurricane said walking toward where he was laying on the ground.

"What? Where's my brother? What have you done with him? If you've hurt him, I'll kill you," Chuck replied.

"Now, Chucky, is that any way for you to talk to the only man who knows where your brother is? Besides, as far as killing me, it doesn't look like you have the upper hand in that either," Sam said as he stepped on one of Chuck's injured legs and retrieved his weapons.

Chuck started screaming from the top of his lungs from the pain. Letting out a series of grunts and gasps, he knew it wasn't a very smart thing to be a tough guy at this point. He humbled himself a little and asked, "How do I know my brother is still alive?"

"Well, Chucky, let me put it this way. He was alive when we left him." Hurricane looked him straight in the eye, "But he's tied up outside in the wilderness, and who knows if any stray animals are having a feast on him right now?"

Chuck knew by the way Hurricane was looking at him that he was telling him the truth, but before he would answer any of his questions, he had one of his own, "If I tell you what I know, will you let my brother and me go?"

"You've got a lot of guts asking such a question, Chucky. But alright, if what you tell me turns out to be what I want, I'll let you and your brother go," Sam agreed, then asked, "Tell me, Chucky, who was the mystery man on the radio a few minutes ago?"

"I can't tell you that. He's crazy, man. He'll hunt me down and kill me," Chuck exclaimed.

"Chucky, I thought we had an agreement. If you change your mind now, I'll put you through so much pain you will beg me to send you to hell," Sam stated.

"You can't do that. I have rights as a citizen of the United States," Chuck muttered.

"You gave up those rights the minute you started conning people out of their life savings and killing their children. Do you see any of these fine officers making a move to stop me? Now, either you start talking, or all hell is going to come crashing down on top of you. I'm getting tired of talking. If you choose to keep silent, I will commence beating you to death. The choice is yours."

Raymond brought Sam's truck into the circle in front of the abandoned school. When Sam opened up the secret compartment of the truck and all of the devices Sam had for causing pain were in view, fear filled Chuck's eyes, and he started opening up, "I'll talk, you crazy bastard. This guy stays somewhere in Milwaukee, but I don't have an exact address. He escaped from prison almost eight months ago, and he's looking for someone who sent him to prison. He won't tell us who he's looking for ... just keeps sending us out to make enough money so he can continue his search," Chuck said.

"Very touching, Chucky, but you left out the most important part so far. What is the man's name?" Hurricane asked intently.

"He calls himself Michael Andrews, but I don't think that's his real name," Chuck answered.

"What prison did he escape from?" Sam asked.

"I think it was Waupun," Chuck answered.

Sam went to his truck, pulled out his computer, and clicked it on. He had impressed the mayor after his help in finding and capturing the murderers in New York, and he was made a member of their elite squad of special agents. That had earned him special computer access to almost any information available on any criminal.

Raymond walked over by Hurricane, and when he saw what Sam was looking at, he couldn't believe his eyes. "Holy cow, Sam. No wonder you're always busy. How do you know which one to go after?" Raymond asked.

"First of all, not all of these criminals are out causing problems. You can tell their status by their designated field. If it's OP, they are out on parole, but the ones in EC are escaped criminals," Hurricane explained.

"What about the ones in DS?" Raymond asked.

"Eventually, they will meet their maker. They have a death sentence," Sam answered. "Hey, now this might be our guy! It says he escaped from Waupun about eight months ago. He just vanished, disappeared from sight. If this is our man, he's been very busy. He's been linked to ten murders in ten different states and stays on the go, never hitting the same place twice. His real name is Sidney Wallace, but he uses several aliases, and one just happens to be Michael Andrews."

Sam noticed that Jimmy's face was pale. Worried, Sam asked, "Jimmy, are you alright? You're as pale as a ghost?"

"You said that killer's name is Sidney Wallace? Are you sure about that?" Jimmy asked.

"Yes, Jimmy, I verified it, and there isn't any doubt that this is the man we are after. Why do you ask?" Hurricane asked.

"That is my real father. Could he really be a killer?" Jimmy was scared. "All I remember is how he used to beat up my mother, sister, and me when he came home drunk."

"Jimmy, I wish I had an answer for you. I was told by a wise old man one time that whenever a person is drunk, his true inner self will show. Whether this is a true statement, I don't really know. I've known quite a few people who get drunk and become a lot friendlier than before. I've also known people who get very loud and disturbing to others. Every now and then, you get a person who is always trying to pick a fight. I don't know what category your father would have fallen under, but I'd wager a good amount of money that he was more than able and may have killed all of you if he hadn't been stopped. You did what you had to do at the time to save your family. I commend you for your honesty and bravery when you were on the stand testifying against your dad," Hurricane told Jimmy.

"What would possess anybody to kill another person?" Jimmy asked.

"If you ever find out the answer to that question, please let me know.

I've had way too many scrapes with people who have raped, kidnapped, or even killed people," Sam replied.

"Why would he come here, and how did he find us?" asked Jimmy.

"I think he's been looking for you ever since he escaped from prison. He blames you for putting him behind bars, instead of realizing it was totally his own fault. I believe he's been traveling from state to state trying to find you. Along the way, he's needed fast money to keep going, so he found people to help him out. Unfortunately, he made the bad mistake of killing the people he captured instead of letting them go, and for that, he must pay the ultimate price of being on the receiving end of death himself," Hurricane responded.

"He's already found me. I'm right here," Jimmy said. "He doesn't have to look any further or kill anyone else. His family is all right here."

"He was probably never told who you are and probably did not know what state your family lived in. Besides, your last name was changed, and he wasn't aware of that. Your mother married Raymond and changed her last name and your sister's as well. I'd bet he never had a clue that his own daughter was almost killed by his men. Had he known he may have been down here himself to do the honors, and she would have already been dead, along with the rest of your family," Hurricane speculated.

"There must be some way of stopping him before any more people get hurt or killed." Jimmy's voice trailed off.

"Your father has finally met his match, Jimmy!" Hurricane said. "When he attacked your family, he was going after my family as well. Raymond and I are like brothers, so he made one fatal mistake. He picked on the wrong family to mess with. Now it's time he met the Hurricane," Sam said.

"That's going to be easier said than done, Hurricane," Jason said. "We don't even know where he is. How are we going to find him?"

Sam never said a word as he looked straight at Chuck and took two steps toward him. Chuck saw the look in Hurricane's eyes and knew he was going to be asked questions for which he didn't have answers. Maybe Carl or Jerry knew where he was. But would they tell Sam, or take the beating, which was going to be brutal? Chuck knew Sam wasn't a dumb man. He wanted answers, and he was going to get them any way he had to.

Sam walked down to his truck, opened the tailgate, and brought back a black bag. He heard some gasps when the three captives noticed the big bolt cutter Sam took out of the bag. It still had blood on it from his last encounter with Chuck's brother.

Sweat started pouring down their foreheads as Sam finally said, "Well, Chucky, you could have possibly saved your brother's life, but by now he has probably lost too much blood and could possibly even be dead. You see, we met your brother Louie and two of his buddies before we arrived here. He was a very quiet fellow and didn't want to talk either until he lost his toes. He may have bled to death already," Sam said.

"You're a barbarian! How could you do that to him?" Chuck asked, starting to cry.

"Let's just say he'll be able to fit into a smaller size shoe. But you shouldn't be too concerned over what he went through. Your concern should be on what I intend to do to you if you don't tell me what I want to know," Sam said with a sinister smile.

Chapter Sixteen

Sam was in no mood to be fooled with. He wanted answers, and he wanted them now. He slowly walked over to Chuck and looked down. Then he wandered over to Jerry.

"I'm going to ask you once very slowly so you understand my question, and if I have to repeat myself, I'll make sure that where you go when you die, it will feel like a relief no matter how hot it gets down there. Now, gents, where can I find your boss, Sidney Wallace, or Michael Andrews, or whatever he calls himself now?"

Carl spoke up, "No matter what you do to us, it is nothing to what he'll do if we tell you anything."

Sam opened up the car door. He grabbed Jerry's right arm clamping down on his wrist. Slowly, Jerry's hand extended outward full open. Sam moved his hand inside the door opening of the car and slammed the door shut. Jerry's fingers where hanging limp as if the bones were detached from his hand when Sam opened the door again. Jerry was screaming from the pain. Still not hearing answers to his question, Sam grabbed his left arm and did the same thing again. When the door was slammed, Jerry almost passed out from the pain. Hurricane threw some cold water on him and brought him to.

Now that he was getting their full attention, he walked over to Carl. As he walked, he spotted a broken tree limb on the ground. He bent down and picked it up. Carl made a fatal mistake and said, "Big man has to use a stick to do his work?"

Sam said, "This big stick you see is about three inches around with a smaller limb broken off at the bottom. You may think it will be used as a weapon, but in fact, it will be used for leverage."

Hurricane lifted Carl's leg and positioned it in the V of the stick. Before Carl could ask what he was doing, Hurricane lifted his right foot and brought it down fast and hard on Carl's ankle, popping the bone out of his skin.

"You see, scumbag, everything isn't as it seems, but I bet you realize that now," Sam said. Carl was lying there writhing in pain. Sam raised the tree limb up toward his knee cap. "Are you ready yet to give me an answer?"

About that time, Raymond said, "Sam, I bet you can't take his hip off like you did that guy back in the service days." It sounded like a challenge.

Carl thought they were kidding until Hurricane spun, bringing his back heel against the limb and striking his knee cap. Carl felt his hip tear from his upper body. He had never felt pain like he was feeling now. Carl's left knee popped from his upper thigh. He knew it was completely separated from his body. He didn't know how much more of this he could take. He knew they had definitely met their match tonight.

Carl was about to start talking when Hurricane turned toward Chuck and walked away. "Why should I let *him* off easy?" Carl thought to himself. "He could have saved all of us a lot of pain if he'd just told them what he knows." Carl also wanted to see what else this madman had up his sleeve. He sure knew how to dish out pain. He also knew just when to stop and make you think about what could be next.

Hurricane walked over to Chuck who was lying on the ground with a bullet hole in both of his legs. Taking out a short drinking straw from his coat pocket, he inserted it into the hole in his leg. Then he pulled out a tube-shaped container and poured it into the straw.

Chuck started screaming as the stuff entered his wound. When Carl saw the label, it was pure salt being inserted into an open wound. He squirmed knowing how painful that was, and then Hurricane pulled another bottle out of his pocket, opened it and began to pour that into the open wound. Chuck started to cry out, "Man, you're killing me!"

Sam smiled, "Chucky, this is only peroxide to keep you from getting infection in your wound. Oh, look at that, the label says not to put it into open wounds as it may cause severe pain. So sorry, Chucky!" Hurricane's tone changed, "However, this is just the beginning. I think you know everything I want to know. If you think you're in pain now ... well, this is nothing compared to the pain you'll have when I start cutting off your toes."

Sam started to rip Chuck's shoes off his feet, but Chuck tried to crawl away. Sam swung around and stuck his broken limb right through the hole in Chuck's leg. Then he turned and looked into Chuck's eyes. Chuck was sweating as he looked at the bolt cutter Hurricane was holding. "Let's see if you are as tough as your brother Louie, shall we? He was one of the toughest I've encountered so far. He lasted until all of his toes were gone," Hurricane said, standing above Chuck holding the bolt cutters open. He was ready to proceed and slowly started to close the cutters over his little toe. He acted like he was having a hard time trying to cut off the toe.

Starting to laugh, Carl showed his ignorance and made a stupid statement toward Hurricane, "What a moron. That bolt cutter isn't even sharp enough to do the job."

Hurricane turned his attention back to Carl. Carl raised his hand to block the sun from his eyes as Hurricane walked over to him. When Hurricane saw this, he raised the cutters and cut off three of Carl's fingers. "Hey, look at that. All I had to do was push the little button to release the safety lock. Am I an idiot or what?" Hurricane asked. Carl was once again in severe pain and was trying frantically to stop the bleeding from where his fingers used to be.

Chuck knew Hurricane meant business. It was either tell him or get taken apart piece by piece. Just as Hurricane started closing the cutters on Chuck's foot, he yelled out, "Okay, I'll tell you what you want to know. Just don't cut us up anymore."

"Tell you what, Chucky, you tell me what I want to know, and I promise I will not cut you up anymore," Sam said.

"He's holed up in a building right off of the Interstate on the Seven Mile Road. It's west off of Highway Ninety-Four. I think the sign said Seven Mile Fairgrounds. There are a few buildings on the land. I'm not sure which one he's in, but it has to have a phone hookup and easy access for a fast getaway," Chuck told Hurricane nervously.

"Is there any other place he could be besides on the fairgrounds?" Hurricane asked.

"Well, that was the only empty place we found. There were a couple of businesses operating, but that would have been too noisy and busy. I'm pretty sure that is the place he'll be. He's getting ready to leave because he thinks our job is done," Chuck answered.

Sam handed Chuck the radio, "Call him. Tell him you had a couple of flat tires, and you'll be a little late." Chuck did as he was told, and they got a fix on his location.

Sam grabbed his gun and tossed the bolt cutters to U.S. Marshal Chester, "He's all yours, boys. I promised I wouldn't hurt him any more. I never mentioned anything about you guys. I'll call you when we have Wallace, aka Michael Andrews."

Chapter Seventeen

After checking the map of Racine County, Hurricane figured it was only five or six miles to the fairgrounds from where they were. He motioned for the other guys as they climbed into the truck. Jimmy ran toward the truck and tried to enter. Sam quickly exited the driver's seat and said, "Jimmy, I know your intentions are good, but this guy is trying to find you. If he knows you are with us, we may not be able to take him alive."

"I want him to die, Sam. He's not my father. He's a cold-blooded killer who must be stopped, and I want to be a part of stopping him," Jimmy told him.

"You're already a big part of the rescue team, son. I'd just feel a lot better if you were somewhere away from here, just in case a bullet should find you. I couldn't live with myself if you became seriously hurt," Sam tried to convince Jimmy.

"I'm also the reason he went to prison, and I'd like to send him back there. So if I witness what happens out there, maybe I'll put him back in for life," Jimmy stated.

Sam had a hard time believing he could talk Jimmy into staying back here with the others. Was his hatred that deep, or was he just curious to see what was going to happen? Sam knew he shouldn't let him go, but he signaled him to enter the truck. Now all he had to do was try to keep him away from the action until it was safe.

Hurricane sped down the road and saw the lock of worry on Jason's face. "Relax, Jason," he said. "This vehicle has a very good suspension system, plus the wheel base is made to withstand this kind of speed without tipping over, or so they say. Just remember who I bought this baby from. They don't buy junk," Sam concluded.

"That's what worries me. If this truck is as good as you say, then why did you buy it from the army surplus lot of broken trucks?" Jason asked.

"I didn't exactly get a second-hand truck," Sam answered.

"But you said you saw it in the junk yard of the military base. Am I right? Jason asked.

"I saw it there, but my comrade replaced the old truck for a brand new one. He just changed the numbers, labels, and paperwork from the old crate to the new crate. I added a few more features to help accommodate me in my line of business. Let's just say he owed me a favor that was paid in full," Hurricane responded.

Hurricane made a wide left turn as he almost passed up the Seven Mile Road. Now the other three guys were a bit worried as well. About half a mile past the turn off, they hit some train tracks that were built up on a little hill. The truck soared through the air and landed with a bounce on the oversized tires. It would have been okay if Sam had been driving the speed limit, but he was hitting eighty-five miles per hour. As soon as they landed, a squad car pulled up behind them.

Sam had no choice but to stop. He didn't want Andrews to get nervous feet at this point and leave. Sam slowed down and pulled over to the edge of the road. The officer walked up to the window and asked for a driver's license and registration.

"Officer Todd Kopecky, this is indeed an honor," Sam said.

"Do I know you, sir?" Officer Kopecky asked.

"Yes, you stopped us once already today. Remember, I was on a case with my men," Sam said.

"Yes, now I remember. I suppose you're on another case now, right?" the officer asked.

"As a matter of fact we are, and if you would like to help us, we could sure use you," Sam said.

"Where are you headed so fast?" Officer Kopecky asked.

Sam explained why they were headed this way, and why he was driving that fast. Officer Kopecky opened up and said, "You know, we checked out a silent alarm there just last week, but by the time we arrived, it had stopped. We drove around the perimeter but didn't see anything. How did he do it without us seeing him or his car?" Officer Kopecky asked.

"What I was told was that he used to work there. He may possibly know the codes, as well as all of the combinations to enter the buildings," Hurricane answered.

"That would make sense," the officer replied.

"I guess he figured by the time you officers would reach this place, he'd be long gone down the highway and out of sight," Hurricane answered, then added, "Now, Officer, would you be willing to help capture this killer, or are you planning on keeping us here so he can get away again?" Hurricane asked.

"I'm all yours, Mr. Rufus. Let me know how I can assist you," Kopecky answered.

"First of all, my friends call me 'Sam' or 'Hurricane.' Second, get as many black and whites as you can assemble together. When we get into the fairgrounds, Jimmy will come back and tell you. Give us about thirty minutes, and then drive into the fairgrounds with your sirens blaring," Hurricane said.

"I thought you didn't want to spook him, Sam. So why are we coming in with our sirens blaring?" Kopecky asked.

"Thirty minutes should give us plenty of time to track him down, but just in case we can't find him, your sirens may spook him enough to come out of hiding and out into the open where we can spot him. Just remember, he's armed and very dangerous. You tell your buddies to be extra careful and take all necessary precautions. He's killed enough people already. I'd hate to see any more good men go down because of him," Hurricane said.

"Understood, Hurricane. As soon as you leave, I'll start setting things up. You guys just watch your backs in case he has guards on the grounds," Officer Kopecky said.

"Todd, you might be right about that. I just took it for granted from his comrades that he was alone. Well, we will soon find out. We are just too close to back away now. Besides, we have all you good County Mounties to help us. I figure if I drive the speed limit, it will take me ten to twelve minutes to reach the fairgrounds. Is that enough time to assemble your troops?"

"We'll be ready to go. Just give us the word, and your new cavalry will come riding in," Officer Kopecky answered with a wide smile on his face.

Hurricane and Officer Kopecky shook hands, and as soon as Sam was in the truck, Todd was on his radio calling for help without saying what he needed help with. He knew that the guy in the warehouse may also have a radio with him, and he could be monitoring police activity.

Sam noticed that he met at least four squad cars as he approached the fairgrounds. He looked around as they passed it up.

Jason said, "Sam, I counted at least six, maybe seven, cameras. If those are on, it will not be as easy as we think."

Sam pulled into an empty parking lot about a block past the entrance to the fairgrounds. He, Jason, Frank, and Raymond walked around to the back of the truck. Sam grabbed two gallon jugs of water and poured them into the dirt. As soon as he had mud, the four guys smeared it all over their faces, hands, and arms. Sam then opened the back of the truck, pushed a button, and the trunk raised up revealing a stash of weapons. Raymond wasn't a bit surprised, but the other guys were in shock. Sam handed them each a shoulder bag containing ten rifle clips, four hand grenades, and a big knife. Jason and Frank watched as Sam and Raymond loaded up with little throwing knives and ninja stars. They all grabbed an AK-47. Then Sam opened up a side compartment and handed each of them some night vision glasses with straps that they could wear around their necks.

"What are these for, Sam? It's still daylight?" Jason asked.

"When we kill the power and enter the building, it may be too dark to see in there. So, as a precaution, let's take them," Sam answered.

Everyone agreed without saying anything more until Sam spoke up, "Well, men, this is it. Jimmy, give us five minutes and then head back to Todd. Jason, after we cut the power, you and Raymond go right, Frank and I will head left. Watch your backs and each other's. We don't exactly know what we are walking into, but we'll soon find out. After this is over, I might have to get a beer."

"After this is over," Raymond said, "Frank and I will throw you guys the biggest party we can. You gave us our families back. We owe you big time." Frank seconded the motion.

"Jason, you heard about that party at Frank and Raymond's house after this is over, so let's get going, shall we? Remember, Jimmy, give us five minutes, then go for reinforcements," Hurricane said.

He looked toward Jimmy who nodded his head in a yes motion as he started the countdown on his watch. Jimmy now understood what Hurricane was trying to tell him before. He might not have been any good at shooting someone, but he was glad he came for the simple fact that all four guys were able to enter the fairgrounds. If he wasn't there, who would they have to drive back for help, and who would have been alone without a partner? They were much safer in numbers. Jimmy looked at his watch. Two minutes had already passed. His adrenalin was going two-forty as the time wound down.

Chapter Eighteen

Jimmy was off and driving as soon as five minutes had ticked by on his watch. As he was passing by the fairgrounds, the lights went out. He knew they would soon be in place. He had to hurry back. His mind drifted back to what Hurricane had said about them going in blind and not knowing what they were up against. His foot almost automatically pushed down on the accelerator. He wasn't even concentrating on how fast he was going.

Within a few minutes, Jimmy thought he was dreaming. The crowd of police cars was up ahead. Not only were the County Officers there, but there were patrol cars from the entire Racine area. They had cars from Racine, Mount Pleasant, Sturtevant, Burlington, Union Grove, and Waterford, not to mention the Highway Patrol Troopers, along with U.S. Marshal Chester Mitchell and his posse from the other ten states involved. They started cheering when they spotted Jimmy driving toward them. They knew that within a few minutes, one more madman would be off the streets.

Marshall Mitchell and Officer Kopecky approached Jimmy, and he gave them the thumbs up as a sign that everything was going as planned. Then Jimmy explained to them about the lights being off and that Hurricane wasn't sure how many others might be involved.

Mitchell and Kopecky were discussing plans to get a little closer in case anything should happen that Hurricane would need them earlier than planned. Todd mentioned the open space before the highway underpass. Because of the underpass, it was blocked from view from the other side.

After finally deciding about how to get closer and where to go, Marshal Mitchell and Officer Kopecky started rounding up the men and explained what was going on. Highway Patrolman Bill Barnes spoke up, "Not to interrupt your plan, but we could always stage a speeding trap up on the highway and view what's going on. If the perps are watching, it could distract them away from what's going on in the building."

"That just might work," Marshal Mitchell said, looking pleased. "They wouldn't suspect that anything was going on except that it's a speeding stop."

"Let's get in place first," Officer Kopecky stated, and then turned to Jimmy, "Jimmy, you all set to be stopped by Patrolman Bill Barnes for speeding?"

"Just tell me what I have to do, and I'm there. Anything to help out, Officer," Jimmy answered. "Can I ask you how you were able to get this many blue and brown shirts together in such a short time?" Jimmy asked, not being able to hold back any longer.

"Well, Jimmy, it seems the girls you left behind were busy calling every law enforcement establishment in the surrounding area. They told them if somebody should call them for help not to ignore it and explained why. I was as surprised as you when all my comrades arrived to give us a hand, but I'm awfully glad they are here. Maybe when that rat perp sees there is no escape, he'll give himself up. The girls and their parents are the real heroes, as far as I'm concerned. Instead of sitting back and waiting, they sent the cavalry," Officer Kopecky stated.

"Let's get set up." Marshal Mitchell yelled. "Time is running short."

They all agreed and started driving down the road, squad car after squad car. People couldn't believe their eyes when they saw the procession of law enforcement vehicles passing by. The owner of the restaurant ran out when he saw car after car pulling into his parking lot. When they explained that it was police business and it would only be a few minutes, he politely nodded his head yes and wished them good luck, even though he walked back into his building shaking his head and muttering to himself.

When all of the cars were in the lot, Marshall Mitchell and Officer Kopecky asked them for some suggestions. Officer Rogers from Racine suggested, "We could stage a car chase past the fairgrounds and set some troops up on the other side. That way they couldn't escape behind them. We could set up in the lot by the Auto Auction business in the back. Then he'd really be locked in the fairgrounds."

Jimmy was going to be real busy for a few minutes. Since he had the only unmarked car there, he was the person who would be chased. He would race down Seven Mile Road right past the fairgrounds with about six squads chasing him. Then he would cut off onto the frontage road with six squads in hot pursuit. Suddenly, three Patrol Troopers on the highway would cut across and stop him. With everyone in place, all they had to do was wait.

When Marshal Mitchell looked at his watch, he noticed that time had slipped by fast with all of the planning they were doing. They would only have to wait another fifteen minutes before entering the fairgrounds. It's funny, but the final few minutes would seem like an eternity, especially since they would be going into a possible gunfight.

While Jimmy and the cavalry were setting up for the charge, Hurricane and his companions were getting ready to enter the building.

Using hand signals, Hurricane indicated they took out five guys. Jason and Raymond indicated one. Only five more to go, Frank motioned with his hands. Jason and Raymond shook their heads no, and then indicated that they had seen eight or ten bodies in the back of the building. Not knowing if they saw the same men, they took precautions just in case there were more than they thought.

"We are sitting in a good spot to see all of the exits and doors. This place is a lot bigger than I thought. However, I think we'd better wait for our reinforcements before making the next move. Let's take a few moments and relax before round two takes place. Besides, I'd like to be sure of just what we are up against," Hurricane whispered to the men with him.

They all nodded their heads in agreement and sat back to take a breather before the excitement started again. "Now I know how Wyatt Earp and his brothers felt, along with Doc Holiday, at the OK Corral," Jason murmured.

Chapter Nineteen

Raymond and Jason were heading around the back of the building. They put on the night vision glasses so they could see through the darkness. They discovered they could also see red images moving inside the building and figured there were eight to ten people inside. Ever so carefully, they slithered closer and closer to the building. When they were within ten feet of the door, they stopped behind a big bush to plan their strategy for entering the building.

Hurricane and Frank were in the front of the building. They also saw eight to ten people inside. Not knowing if Raymond and Jason had spotted them, they knew they had to move fast.

There was a big storage shed not far from the front entrance. They stopped there to take a breath before making their move. Hurricane motioned to Frank to stay close behind him. They ran up to the door, keeping a low profile. Finding it locked, they moved down the wall, checking each door. Finally, the door on the end was unlocked. After counting to three by raising their fingers, they swung the door open and slipped inside. With the glasses on, it was easy to see where they were going. They had the upper hand at this moment, but this building was big. At the pace they were moving, the posse would be here before they were ready.

Frank indicated to Hurricane that they split up and go down each aisle and meet in the middle. Hurricane nodded in agreement, and they went their own way.

For the first two or three aisles it was quiet. Then they came upon two men sitting on a bench on the end aisle. Hurricane stood upright and walked around the far end. One of the men tried to get up, but before he could stand, Hurricane dropped him to the floor. The other guy pulled a gun out of his coat and pointed it at Hurricane. Just then, Frank jumped up and hit the guy in the back of the head with his gun. As he fell toward the floor, Frank turned the gun at the other guy and signaled for him to get rid of his gun. About that time, another guy farther down saw the commotion and was about to head down there. Frank looked around for Hurricane, but he was not in sight. When Frank looked back toward the man, he was on the floor in a pool of blood. Then he felt a tap on his shoulder. Frank turned his head and saw Hurricane standing there. In that brief moment, his prisoner tried to run and then hit the ground. Just like that, Hurricane had thrown one of his knives, hitting the man in the back of the head. He was dead.

Frank was dumbfounded that Sam could move so fast that he never even saw the knife leave his hand. But, of course, it was dark inside the building, and those glasses took away their side vision.

Hurricane signaled four down and seven to go, counting the big man. Frank nodded in the affirmative.

They split up again and continued through the aisles. After six rounds, they found themselves by the bathrooms. Sam signaled to go in and check the rooms. First, they went into the men's room. Nothing. As they were about to exit, they heard footsteps and hid in the toilet stalls. The door opened, and they heard a guy running toward the urinals. When he started going, Sam quietly moved up behind him. Just as he finished, Hurricane snapped his neck and down he went.

"Hey, Joe, did you fall asleep in there?" someone called.

Hurricane hid behind the door as it slowly opened, and the person came in. When he saw his friend on the floor, he called out, "Hey, Joe, are you okay? Just get up, and stop joking around." Just then, Frank came out of the toilet stall. "Who the heck are you, and how did you get in here?" the stranger demanded.

"You know, it never hurts when you don't see it coming," Frank said.

"What are you talking about, mister? I ..." Just before he finished his sentence, Hurricane stuck a knife through his ribs, killing the man instantly.

"Six down, four to go," Frank said silently. "Let's go get the others, shall we?"

While Hurricane and Frank were having their fun, Raymond and Jason had a few things happening on their end. After finding out that all of the doors in the back were locked, they noticed a red glow inside one of the doors. Jason knocked on the door. As the person inside opened it, Raymond grabbed his arm and yanked him outside. Jason stuck his gun barrel in the bottom of the door to keep it open. Jason went over to help Raymond, but he was too late. The stranger lay on the ground in a pool of blood.

"Let's go exploring, shall we," Raymond suggested.

They nodded their heads yes and entered the building, glad they had the glasses Sam had given them. They proceeded in the same way Sam and Frank were exploring and split up. As they rounded the third row of display booths, Jason noticed one guy sleeping inside a booth. He was sleeping in one of those massage chairs and never heard Jason sneak up on him. As his head was held tight, a knife was stuck in his back through the chair.

After three more rows, they both heard a noise. Very slowly, they rounded the turn and saw two men. Just as they were about to strike, they came face to face with Hurricane and Frank.

Hurricane and his friends sat inside the building resting and waiting for the posse to arrive. Kopecky, Mitchell, and company were preparing for the big charge. Every officer involved was ready to strike. As long as the power was off, Mitchell thought it wouldn't hurt to open all of the gates, not only for easier access, but to get really close to the building as well. When the final gate was opened, it was time. Officer Kopecky yelled that magic word on the radio, "NOW!"

Within seconds the sirens were so loud that all of Chicago could have heard them. They advanced on the building so fast that the bad guys had no chance to escape. It was either surrender or die.

Jason was a bit startled as he said, "Sam, do you hear all of those sirens? It sounds like the whole police force is out there."

"Yes, Jason, I hear them, and it all sounds like music to my ears. We have to get ready to make our move," Hurricane said. "First, we will just wait here for a few seconds and see what happens."

Chapter Twenty

Just as Hurricane finished with what he was saying, a door swung open and several guys scattered, looking for a safe spot to hide. They were all heavily armed with automatic rifles and ammunition as they spread out for a gunfight.

They were so worried about finding a place to sit down that nobody even noticed Hurricane and company sitting in front of them. Sam handed each of his guys a pair of ear plugs. It was going to get a bit noisy, and he wanted them to be prepared for battle.

Before they inserted the ear plugs, Hurricane said, "We have one thing in our favor. They don't know we're here."

"I think they'll find out soon enough, my friend," Raymond stated.

"How many more of these guys are here? I think we may have bitten off more than we can chew," Jason spoke out.

"This time, we stay together and watch each other's backs," Hurricane remarked, and then added, "Shall we go join the party, my friends?"

"Heck!" Raymond exclaimed, "I forgot the ice cream. Let's go take care of business."

They were getting ready to advance toward the enemy when the door suddenly opened again. Four more guys came running out. Hurricane motioned for them to enter that door and see how many more may be inside. When they were all in the room, they were staring at a big, open bank vault. Sam wasn't sure if it had been open, or if they opened it, but now he knew why they couldn't see all of these guys through the walls.

The glasses could only penetrate through wood and metal, but not solid steel like these vaults were made of. The room was now empty. Hopefully, there would be no more surprises.

They exited the room two by two, just in case they bumped into some unexpected company. As they were advancing toward their first target, shots rang out and bullets started flying everywhere. "How many cops are out there?" Hurricane asked himself. They started to crawl toward the exit doors. They spotted four guys sitting by the ammunition boxes loading clips for the shooters. Hurricane made an evil smile as he looked back toward the guys. He took out two hand grenades, pulled the pins, and rolled them toward the boxes. The noise around them drowned out the sound of them rolling across the floor. They stood up and ran back toward the other side of the building. Within ten seconds, the blast rang out, leaving a hole in the side of the building big enough to drive a tank through. Bullets were flying everywhere as the ammo boxes exploded.

Hurricane and the boys stood up and started shooting anyone they saw who was left.

Suddenly, they heard a booming voice behind them, "So you're the bastards causing us all of this goddamn grief!"

As the guys turned, they saw what looked like a dozen men holding guns on them. Knowing they were in deep trouble, they dropped their weapons and waited for their next step.

"Hey, coppers. I have four of your men. If you don't back off, I'll kill them all," the man they assumed was Sidney Wallace bellowed.

The gunfire ceased, and a voice could be heard, "You are surrounded. There is no escape. Let those officers go, and walk out with your hands raised."

"To whom am I speaking?"

"I'm U.S. Marshal Chester Mitchell," he answered. "May I ask to whom I am speaking?"

"Michael Andrews," he answered. "Now that we are buddies, back your men up, or we will start killing these men."

"I don't think you are that stupid, Michael Andrews, or Sidney Wallace, or whatever name you are going by now. As long as they are alive, we will not rush you. If you kill your hostages, what do you think we will do? Let's see if we can't negotiate, and maybe nobody gets hurt. What do you say?"

Marshal Chester Mitchell asked.

"I see you have done your homework, Marshal. I am impressed. You must have also found out that I never surrender, which means I don't care if these prisoners live or die," Wallace said. After a few moments of silence, he asked, "What, Marshal, cat got your tongue? Or are you thinking we have the upper hand?"

"I must say you do have us in a small dilemma, but I really don't think you want to die today. If you send out two of your prisoners we will consider pulling back a little," Marshal Mitchell replied.

"The only way I'll send them out is in body bags, Marshal. Now, why don't you stop playing games and back your men up so we can slip by you?" Andrews asked.

While the two men were negotiating, Hurricane managed to pass a few knives to his teammates. Wallace and his men had not tied them up yet and were more interested in the dozens of lawmen they were facing.

The four men slowly separated a bit, so they would have room to move. Then like a precision group of guys who had been together for years, they twirled around and, at the same time, cut the throats of several of Wallace's men and disappeared from view just as fast.

Nobody followed Hurricane and his men because they were too busy trying to help their buddies. They had not bothered to frisk Hurricane or his men. Hurricane opened his coat and revealed several hand guns—three semi-automatic pistols with several clips for each, two .45 caliber and two .357 Magnum pistols. He had plenty of ammunition for quite a while. After distributing the weapons, they figured they would split up the posse and watch the whole area. Each of them went their own way as Wallace was busy berating his own men for letting them escape.

Hurricane knew that when the first shot rang out, there would soon be encores, with even more bullets flying in from the outside. It seemed strange that four guys could surround at least twenty or so men. Many others had either died or were badly wounded when the grenades went off. Thinking of the grenades, Hurricane checked and still had at least four left. There was little doubt that he would use them if needed.

With the big hole now in the wall, they didn't need the night vision glasses. Raymond saw the tops of at least three heads moving his way. He steadied his wrist and took aim in their direction. As soon as one poked his head up, Raymond fired. He was a marksman like Hurricane in the Marines. He never forgot how to shoot. Just as they would poke out their heads, Raymond would fire his weapon. They ducked as bullets started flying inside the building. Several of the bad guys were hit, but there was no way to know how badly they were wounded. It couldn't be good. Bullets were flying for at least four or five minutes, and then there was silence.

Hurricane managed to move within arm's reach of the group of men he was facing. He picked up a ceramic dog that was on the table and threw it, hitting one man in the back of the head. The man rubbed his head and made the mistake of going to find out where it came from by himself. When he arrived at the area from which it had been thrown, he found nobody there. As soon as he put his safety on and dropped his weapon, Hurricane jumped up and stuck his knife in his throat so he couldn't speak. "Never put your safety on in the middle of a battle," Hurricane said softly toward the man as he died in his arms.

Jason was on his own now, and he was shaking as he ventured toward the open hole in the wall. When he arrived, he saw four men lying on the floor. Three were dead, and one was barely holding on. When their eyes made contact, the man on the floor motioned to him that men were in the next aisle. He blinked four times, and Jason figured he was telling him how many were there. "Why would he want to help me?" Jason asked himself. He slowly crawled around the corner, and bingo, there they were. Jason cocked his weapons and made a lunge toward the open aisle. He emptied his weapons, hitting three of them before he ran out of ammo. Just when he thought he was a dead man, a shot rang out, and the fourth man hit the ground. He was stunned as he looked behind him and saw a blue uniform standing outside the opening. Jason waved to say thanks as he crawled back toward the aisle to reload.

More officers entered the building to assist.

Meanwhile, Hurricane was still throwing things as he spotted another group of guys standing in a circle. Slowly, he pulled the pin on a grenade, released the handle, waited about three seconds, and tossed it toward the group. All of them went down as the grenade exploded Hurricane crawled over to make sure they were dead. Four of them had been able to crawl away, but they left a trail of blood. Hurricane was smiling as he went after them. If they were bleeding as badly as it appeared, they wouldn't get very far. The trail led into the bathroom.

"Why do I always get the bathroom jobs?" he asked himself. Slowly, he opened the door and saw three of the four men lying on the floor in front of him. They weren't moving, so he crawled over to them to see if they were dead. One of the men made a move at Hurricane, but he was so weak he couldn't hold on. Hurricane looked toward the divider that separated the toilet from the urinals and saw a shadow coming toward him. He spun around just as the man lunged at him with a knife in his right hand. Unfortunately for him, Hurricane was also holding a knife. As the attacker fell on top of him, he stuck the knife into the man's stomach. He had to block the stranger's right arm that held the knife to keep from being stabbed.

Raymond was having his own share of trouble. After shooting the first man, the other three split up. Looking up, Raymond noticed that there were round mirrors in the aisles. He would use them to his advantage. Ray noticed a shadow coming around the corner and dropped to his back to take aim. When the intruder peeked around the corner, he never had time to move, as the bullet penetrated his forehead.

Raymond felt like he was in the shooting gallery at the county fair, waiting for the ducks to show their heads. He knew there were at least two more. "Where can they be?" he thought to himself, trying to listen for some sort of noise. Between the ear plugs and the gunfire all around the area, it was difficult to hear anything. Raymond decided to use what they used to call "covert tactics." It was pretty easy to rig things up, and then he hid in the back of the display booth.

He didn't have to wait long. The next man found one of his "dropped" ear plugs on the floor and saw a shoe sticking out from under the table of the booth Raymond was hiding in. He reached to pick up the shoe, but it was caught on something. When he pulled harder, it triggered a rubber band to spring forward like a slingshot carrying a knife that hit the bad guy right between his eyes. "Three down. Only one more to go, hopefully," Raymond said to himself.

He dragged the body out of sight and decided to set up another booby trap for the next guy. Raymond found himself in a booth where the vendor sold knives, switchblades, and swords. "How perfect is this?" he thought to himself, looking for something to set up trap number two. Keeping a low profile and moving quickly, Raymond found a mannequin about his own size and put his shirt on it. He attached a sharp sword and then stretched it around with some strong rubber bands. He found a kid's whirligig and attached it to the mannequin, hoping it wouldn't fall. Just in case, he held onto another sword and waited. It was amazing how long he actually had to set these things up. These guys definitely were not professionals.

Just as he was about to give it up, he saw a shadow creeping toward his area. The man was looking all around, then whispered loudly, "Joey, Jimmy, Roger, come on guys. Quit kidding around. Where are you?" Then he spotted the mannequin. He walked up to it, grabbed its shoulder, and spun it around. He stood there in shock as his arm he was using to hold his gun fell and hit the floor when the attached sword made its swing.

"Surprised?" Raymond asked as he entered the area and stuck him in the heart with his sword. Raymond decided to take the sword with him and found a strap to hold it to his belt.

Frank headed toward the doors. He knew reinforcements were outside waiting to gain entrance. Just a few feet from the big doors, he spotted four men guarding the entrance. Assessing the situation, Frank noticed a big sign hanging over their heads. He traced the ropes holding the sign up and saw they were tied in a dark corner of the building. If he could make it over there, he might be able to take these guys out without firing a shot.

Frank tried crawling under tables but found that most of the fair display booths had separating walls. Carefully, he began worming his way toward the corner and eventually found himself where he wanted to be. He tugged on the ropes to find out which one he had to untie first. The bottom rope was pretty easy. Because of the weight of the sign and the pressure, the top rope was going to be a lot harder to untie.

Frank remembered the knives Hurricane had given them. He took one out and slowly started to cut the rope, being careful not to cause the sign to move. That knife was so sharp it cut the thick rope like butter. Only two strands remained, the only thing holding the sign up. Frank decided the only way to do this was to cut it fast. He raised his arm and brought the knife down hard, cutting the last two strands. The sign came down like a guillotine and took out all four guys. Frank couldn't believe he had hit all four of them at once, but he was very happy.

Just as he walked over to the doors, the power came back on inside the building. Frank hit the open button, and the big doors started rising. Looking out, he stood in amazement at the sight of all the police cars outside.

Suddenly, a gunshot rang out and snapped him back to reality. Ducking and turning, he spotted Jason standing behind him with his gun pointed toward the floor. On the floor lay a gunman with a bullet in his head. Frank realized that Jason had just saved his life. He had to stay focused until this thing was over.

Chapter Twenty-One

Hurricane was on a mission to find Sidney Wallace, aka Michael Andrews. He was so wrapped up in finding his prey that he broke his own cardinal rule and let his guard down. He stood up and walked toward the closed door. Before he was halfway there, what looked like fifteen bad guys circled around him. Sam realized he was in the middle of a bad situation. One of them, a man about six feet three inches and 350 pounds, walked up to Hurricane and said, "I'm going to crush you, little man."

"You know, you have me at a disadvantage," Hurricane said.

"Why is that?" the man asked.

"Because you know you are bigger than me," Hurricane answered.

"Stronger, too, but what can you do about it, little man?" He asked Hurricane again.

"I guess I'll have to bring you down to my size," Hurricane answered, spinning around and hitting the big man in the knee caps. He hit him so hard and fast that his knees buckled inward as the big man fell straight down. "Gee, that looks like it really hurts," Hurricane said.

The big man couldn't move. "What did you do to me? Make the pain stop," he cried.

Hurricane walked up to him now that they were eye to eye, "You're not so tall anymore, big man. Do you really want me to stop your pain?" He asked.

The big man nodded his head yes.

Hurricane moved fast as he slid a knife out of his jacket and cut the big man's throat. He knew he would have to fight his way out of this one.

"He's only one man. Let's get him!" one of the others yelled.

"Now, now, boys. That just doesn't seem fair to me," Raymond suddenly spoke, standing behind them holding his sword. Sam was very happy to see his old friend.

"Only two of you against us? Who are you kidding?"

"Make that three," Jason called, suddenly appearing out of nowhere.

"No, more like four," Frank called coming toward them. "Hey, guys, are you ready to rumble?"

"Frank, did anybody ever tell you that you watch too much television?" Raymond asked, never moving his eyes from his enemies.

"Only the four of you fighting against all of us! This will not take long," one of the strangers said, laughing.

"You are the ones at a disadvantage. You're about to learn what a real Hurricane feels like," Raymond said.

"What hurricane? This is Wisconsin. We don't have hurricanes. Now, get ready to die."

"You can't say I didn't warn you," Raymond said. Then he swung his sword and took three guys down at the knees with one mighty swipe. "Your friends can now call you 'Stumpy,' " he laughed.

One of the guys tried to fire toward Raymond, but Frank grabbed his arm and pushed him away just as he pulled the trigger. He took out three of his own men.

Jason was busy fighting off three men who tried to grab him. Shots were heard, and two of them hit the floor. Jason hit the third guy in the head with the gun, and he dropped like a rock.

Hurricane was watching how things were developing. He saw Raymond swinging that sword like he was a Musketeer. Frank and Jason were busy helping each other in the far corner.

Hurricane caught a guy trying to sneak up on him, and he swung around so fast it startled the pursuer. He stopped just long enough to look into Hurricane's eyes before he felt a knife pierce his neck. Four more guys tried to rush Hurricane, but he swung his body around with roundhouse kicks, stopping them in their tracks. While they were hunched over, he brought down one of his mighty hammer fists and crushed the ear of one of the men. Then an upper cut with one of his bear paws smashed his teeth and dislocated the guy's jaw.

One of the others tried to get Hurricane with his own roundhouse kick, but Hurricane saw it coming. He dropped to a split, and brought up a thrusting blow full strength. He hit the man so hard between the legs that he likely broke his pelvic bone.

Number four came after Hurricane with a look of vengeance on his face. He was swinging wildly, but each blow was blocked by a more seasoned veteran. After a couple of minutes, the attacker was getting winded and mad. He threw everything at Hurricane that wasn't connected. Hurricane was fooled into thinking he was getting tired, and when Hurricane let down his guard, he gave Hurricane a straight punch in the face, causing blood to flow from his nose. He tried to quickly hit him again. Hurricane not only blocked his punch but grabbed his hand and started to squeeze. The attacker went to his knees as Sam crushed the bones in his fingers. He looked in Hurricane's eyes and screamed. What he saw was death—his own. Just as he screamed, Hurricane hit the man under the bridge of his nose. The impact was so hard it pushed his nose up into his skull and killed him instantly.

Hurricane spotted a couple of bad guys on top of a wall waiting to jump on Raymond. Hurricane yelled his name and pointed up. Raymond stuck his sword straight up instantly without even looking and caught one of them in the heart as he fell right on top of him. Raymond lost his grip on the sword. Spotting it, the second guy was about to jump for it just as shots rang out. Hurricane and Raymond looked toward the area where the shots originated and spotted thirty or so blue and brown shirts running their way.

Frank and Jason were too busy to notice. They were battling six bad dudes of their own until a few friendly faces stepped in to help. With a surprised look on their faces, they welcomed the much-needed help.

Within thirty minutes tops from the time they had entered the building, the only men standing were Frank, Raymond, Jason, U.S. Marshal Chester Mitchell, Officer Kopecky, Hurricane, and at least seventy of the finest lawmen you could ask for. Hurricane looked around and was amazed, "How in the world did you end up with all of these beautiful officers?"

"Well, it seems that while we were waiting to help you, four women were busy calling every law enforcement station they could find, explaining what was happening. When I made the SOS call for help, all of these special officers showed up," Officer Kopecky explained.

"You have four people deeply in your debt, my friends, and we thank you," Hurricane said

"No, Hurricane, when we heard what you guys were up against, it was our honor to be able to help you get these scumbags off the streets for good," one of the sergeants spoke.

"What is your name, Sergeant?" Hurricane asked

"My name is Sergeant Thomas Matson, at your service, sir," he answered.

"I'm Hurricane, or Sam, Sergeant. You and your men are an inspiration to us all," Hurricane said as he shook his hand.

"I hate to break up this moment, Hurricane, but Wallace isn't here," Jimmy stated.

"He has to be. There's nobody left," Hurricane told him.

"He must have slipped out the back while you were busy fighting his army," Jimmy replied.

"Are you sure, Jimmy? Did you check all of the bodies?" Sam asked. "Maybe you missed him."

"He isn't here, Hurricane. He just isn't anywhere to be found. I wish he was. That madman knows where she lives," Jimmy squawked.

"What do you mean he knows where she lives?" Sam asked. "Do you think he would know the address of your mother's house," Sam asked, "your birth mother, that is?"

"It's a very good possibility, Hurricane. That's why I'm worried," Jimmy answered.

"This may have been a set up. He may have wanted us out of the way so he could get to your mother," Sam said.

"But why would he sacrifice all of his men that he's gathered from ten different states?" Jimmy asked.

"To give him free access to run. This may have all been a ploy to get to your mother and her children," Sam answered.

"Hey, Hurricane, come here quick!" U.S. Marshall Mitchell hollered.

"What wrong, Chester?" Sam asked.

"I've been trying to call Raymond's home number. It's a steady busy tone," Chester answered.

"Where is Raymond?" Hurricane asked.

"He took off in a police car to see if she was alright," Chester said.

Sam tried to get Raymond to answer the police radio. He didn't know if the radio was off or if Raymond just wasn't answering. Sam was pacing like a tiger until Chester said, "Hurricane, we have everything under control here. Why don't you go check on your friend, and if you need help, call us. These guys aren't going anywhere for quit a while."

Sam, Frank, Jason, and Jimmy jumped in the truck and headed for Raymond's house. Hurricane was definitely speeding, but nobody said a word. They were all anxious to end this, for everybody's sake.

Frank was very quiet, not saying a word. He was very worried because his family was probably with Raymond's family.

Hurricane was hoping Raymond wasn't walking into a death scene and his own assassination. He just knew he didn't have time to waste, especially if that madman was there.

Chapter Twenty-Two

Jimmy was beside himself as he asked Hurricane, "Sam, do you think my father knew who I was all along and was using me to find my mother?"

"That's a good possibility, Jimmy, but don't worry. He isn't going to hurt anybody else," Sam replied.

"How can you be so sure of that?" Jimmy asked. "He may have already killed my mother and sister, and now maybe even Raymond."

"Because, if he does, it will be the last thing he will ever do. You have to have faith, my young friend," Sam answered.

"But he may just get jail time again and find us when he gets out," Jimmy fearfully acknowledged.

"Jimmy, will you load my gun, please?" Hurricane asked as he handed Jimmy his .357 Magnum. Jimmy carefully loaded Sam's gun and handed it back to him. He looked into Hurricane's eyes, and it was like he could read his mind. Without saying a word, Jimmy knew his father would be dead. He had never before seen the look that was in Hurricane's eyes. It was almost like the devil himself was in Hurricane's body.

Hurricane slowed down as he approached the house. Instead of parking on Arthur Avenue, he parked around the corner on Kinzie Avenue. He could sneak up on the house a lot easier. Sam opened another compartment on his truck and took out some more ammo clips, tossing them to Frank and Jason. He turned to them, "Do you still have your handguns?" When they nodded yes, he continued, "I'd like you two in the backyard, and if he tries to leave, shoot to kill. This time the only way he leaves us is with a bullet. No matter what, he does not escape. If you wound him, you finish him off." Sam wanted to make it very clear that, by any means necessary, he was to be killed.

Hurricane and Jimmy waited a couple of minutes to give Frank and Jason a chance to get in the backyard. When Sam figured it was time, he patted Jimmy on the back and said, "Party time, Jimmy. Let's go." They both walked on the sidewalk toward the house. When they were in front of the house, they ducked down and crawled up to the front window where the shade was slightly raised. Looking inside, they couldn't believe their eyes. All four women were in their underwear and tied up in chairs. "This is one sick S.O.B.," Sam said out loud.

Wallace walked into the room carrying a bucket of water. He set it down in front of Connie and put her left foot into the bucket. Then he yanked the electric cord out of a lamp and put on a pair of rubber gloves he had found in the kitchen. He plugged the cord into the wall socket and brought the loose end over to the bucket. He took the open wire end and touched it to the water inside the bucket. Connie shook as a big jolt of electricity pierced through her body. Shirley screamed, and Wallace stood there laughing as Connie slowly came back to her senses.

"What's wrong, dear? This is what they threatened to do to me if I ever came near you and the children again. I just wanted to let you know what I almost went through. Now that I believe I have your undivided attention, I'd like you to tell me where our son is," Wallace demanded, his voice growing angry and bitter.

"I don't know where he is. They took him away from me after they put you away," Connie answered.

"Forgive me if I don't believe you. I have to make sure you are telling the truth," Wallace said and lowered the cord to the water once again. This time, he gave her a longer jolt of electricity. When he took it out, he noticed a trace of blood coming from Connie's mouth.

"She's telling the truth, Dad," Shirley screamed, then added. "They were afraid you would go after him when you got out of prison because you threatened to kill him for testifying against you. I haven't seen him since then myself. I wouldn't even know him if I saw him today."

"So, my little girl still calls me 'Dad.' You're all grown up now, a fine-looking specimen," he said, looking Shirley up and down. "Maybe I'll let your mother rest a while and give you a taste of what I do to traitors."

Connie started pleading with him to leave their daughter out of this, but he turned around and backhanded her across the face. He went into the kitchen and came back with a coffee can, matches, and some newspapers. Both ends of the can had been opened. He put a metal pie plate on the floor and taped Shirley's foot to the top end of the open can.

Shirley kicked and fought against what he was doing until the man watching them from the door came in and taped her legs to the chair with some duct tape.

Wallace wadded up the newspaper and set it on fire on the plate and placed the can over the fire. "This may not look too terrible right now, but when the can gets hot enough your skin will start to burn off of your foot. Now tell me where the boy is!" The way Shirley was taped to the chair, she was completely unable to move her foot. All of the women were crying and begging Wallace to stop.

"That's all I can take. I'm going in," Hurricane whispered to Jimmy. Before Jimmy could say a word, Sam went crashing through the window. Wallace was startled to see someone else there. He tried to hit Hurricane with the lamp, but Hurricane ducked and came up with a sharp upper cut, crashing Wallace down on the coffee table.

Jimmy went through the window after Hurricane and put out the fire. He untied Shirley, Anne, and Susan. Just as he was going toward his mother, someone grabbed him from behind and threw him against the wall, knocking the breath out of him, and then kicked him in the jaw. Jimmy fell to the floor and didn't move.

The attacker then turned his attention toward Hurricane and Wallace. Just as Hurricane drew back to hit Wallace with a crushing right hand, someone grabbed his arm and tried to hit him. Hurricane ducked and came up with an upper cut of his own. He sent the intruder crashing against the wall. While Hurricane was distracted, Wallace saw an opportunity and tried to make a run for it out the back door, only to run into a big African American man and a middle-aged white man on the back porch. Before he could say a word, Jason hit him hard, and he went crashing through the door back into the house, landing on the floor.

Jason and Frank went into the house and found Hurricane in a tough fight with a huge Samoan man. He was gigantic, 400 pounds or more. He had Hurricane in a bear hug and was squeezing the air out of him. Hurricane's arms were trapped under the big man's arms. Suddenly, Hurricane flipped backwards taking the giant with him. They went crashing to the floor. Hurricane was trying to draw air into his lungs, while the big giant lay confused and wondering what had just happened.

Jimmy came to and shook his head. Looking around, he saw that his mother was still tied up in the chair. He crawled over and untied her, and she moved against the wall to get out of the way of Hurricane and the Samoan man.

Jason and Frank saw that Sam's fight was under control and turned back to Wallace lying on the floor moaning. They started to pull him up by the collar, but Wallace suddenly smashed Frank in the head with a wooden baton. The blow sent him careening to the floor, tripping Jason in the process. Wallace then turned his attention to Jason.

With the women safely out of the room, Jimmy ran toward his father who was about to bring a hard, striking blow down on Jason. Jimmy lunged at him shoulder first and crashed into Wallace's knees, pushing his kneecap to the side of his leg. Wallace fell to the floor and was instantly in agonizing pain. Jimmy picked up the baton and began striking him, hitting him with all of his might all over his body. "You want me? Well, here I am, *Daddy!*" Jimmy yelled at him as he struck him with the baton. Wallace cried out for Jimmy to stop, but Jimmy unleashed years of hatred onto him.

Since Wallace seemed to be unable to do any more damage, and Jimmy was doing a good job of keeping him occupied, Jason turned his attention once again in Hurricane's direction.

Hurricane had finally found a worthy opponent who could not only take the powerful blows from his heavy hands but who could also deliver his own. The only difference between the two of them was that Hurricane was much quicker than that mighty giant. The big Samoan was hitting Hurricane with blows from his own big hands, and it seemed like Hurricane was actually enjoying this fight. Jason couldn't believe his eyes. He noticed Hurricane smile as he was getting hit. "He truly has a few screws loose," Jason thought to himself.

With every hit the Hurricane received, he seemed to be getting meaner and meaner and was about ready to inflict some serious pain. Both brawlers' hands were covered in blood, and both men had cuts on their faces. And then the big Samoan hit Hurricane in the face, causing his nose to start spurting blood. Jason knew he had gone too far when he saw that look in Hurricane's eyes. Hurricane let out a scary, high-pitched yell, and it was the end of the road for the big giant. Hurricane started working on his knees, giving him a big straight-leg kick right on the knee. There was a cracking sound, and the big giant wasn't as tall anymore. Hurricane grabbed one of his big arms and twisted it, trying to wrench it from his shoulder. With a quick twist, he brought his arm around over his shoulder and brought his elbow straight down so hard the big man's elbow actually popped out of the skin.

Jason was shocked to see just how Hurricane was dismantling this giant of a man. He began to think that Hurricane had just been toying with him before. "Who is this man they call Hurricane?" Jason wondered. "He never seems to tire or feel pain. It's almost like the more pain he receives, the stronger he becomes. Is he really human?" Jason was thinking to himself.

When Jason thought he had seen it all, he couldn't believe what Hurricane did next.

With the big Samoan kneeling on the floor, helpless and unable to stand because of his knee and unable to fight with only one arm, Hurricane walked behind the big giant and started hitting him in the spine. The Samoan was crying in pain as Sam was smashing his fists into his spine.

When Hurricane made it to the back of his head, he walked around to face the big, battered giant and spoke to him, saying, "You were a mighty opponent. I enjoyed our little fight, my big friend. You are only the second man who ever gave me such a problem. I respect you for that. But, unfortunately, one of us will have to leave now. I just wanted you to know this before I kill you."

The big Samoan responded in a pained voice, "You proved to be a mighty warrior, and if I have to die now, I know I have fought a courageous opponent and will die with honor. I'll see you again in another world and maybe we can be friends."

With that said, Hurricane walked around to his back and swung his mighty arm. He hit the giant in the back of the head, breaking his neck and causing instant death.

When the fight was over, Sam slumped over, and for the first time,

Jason knew he felt pain. "Maybe he's human after all," Jason thought as he surveyed the room.

"Hey, Sam, where's Raymond? I haven't seen him since we entered this house," Jason said.

Suddenly, the front door opened, and Raymond came in holding two more guys he had found outside. His shirt was nearly torn off his body, and his face looked swollen, but he was all smiles. At least, they thought they were smiles until he said, "Where were you guys? Here I was outside fighting these two trespassers, and you're in here sitting down? Just what have you been … ?" His voice trailed off as he began to process the scene before him.

"Raymond," Jason started, "let me introduce you to Sidney Wallace, aka Michael Andrews. This is the man who has caused you so much pain. We figured we would save him for you. I think this is real personal between you two."

Raymond's eyes surveyed the room—broken furniture, five men lying on the floor, four chairs with ropes hanging on them, his wife Connie standing in her underwear with dried blood on her lips. "What the …" Raymond muttered, quickly walking to Connie. He cradled her in his arms. "Are you alright, honey?" he asked, looking into her eyes.

Just as Connie nodded yes, Shirley, Anne, and Susan walked into the room and handed a robe to Connie, which she quickly donned. Shirley and Susan had on sweats that he recognized as Shirley's, and Anne was wrapped in a blanket. Raymond's eyes turned to fire as he suddenly figured out what had happened here, and then he spotted the bucket of water and the electric cord.

"You are one sick bastard, Wallace," focusing his attention on the man Jimmy was holding on the floor. "I'm going to make sure you never hurt another soul on this earth," Raymond said.

"And what are you going to do, talk me to death?" Wallace commented sarcastically.

Raymond grabbed the rope that was on the floor and walked over to him. "Get up!"

"I can't. My leg is broken," Wallace snarled.

"Then put your hands behind your back," Raymond ordered.

After he tied Wallace's hands behind his back, he reached down and pulled him up to his feet. "I see you like electricity, aka Andrews," Raymond snarled at him. "Let me show you what it can do when water and steel are mixed together," he said, shoving Wallace into one of the chairs.

Raymond went to the garage and brought in two galvanized steel pipes. He tore Wallace's pant legs and began duct taping the pipes to each of his bare legs, leaving one leg only half taped so the leg could be bent.

Raymond pulled the bucket of water in front of Wallace and lifted his broken leg, placing his foot in the water. Wallace had no strength to pull his leg out. The next thing he saw was Raymond bringing in a 220-volt battery charger that was plugged into a 220-volt receptacle in the garage. He attached the clips from the charger to the ends of the two pipes.

"Are you ready to feel what it's like?" Raymond asked him. "For all of the murders you have caused and all of the pain you have inflicted on those innocent families, as well as for the pain you inflicted on your own wife and children who, by the way, are standing here watching you get your just reward, I hereby sentence you to death by electricity. Do I hear any objections?" he asked.

Just as Wallace was trying to say something, Raymond threw the switch. Instantly, they could smell flesh burning. Wallace was trying to scream, but nothing was coming out, except his mouth and ears were oozing blood. Suddenly, the lights went out, "Damn, tripped a breaker. I'll be right back," Raymond said.

When the lights came back on, Wallace's skin was starting to burn off of his body. "Hey, Wallace, look at you," Raymond said as he came back into the room. He lifted a mirror from the wall and held it in front of Wallace so he could see himself.

"Just kill me and get it over with," Wallace said, turning his head away.

Connie stepped up. "What's wrong, Sidney? Absorbing pain isn't as exciting as inflicting it? Just think about all of the people whose lives you have inflicted with pain. This is called 'payback time.' This time, I'll flip the switch for all you have put us through these past years," Connie said. With that, she reached down and flipped on the switch.

Before Wallace died, he bit his tongue off and then was still. They turned off the charger and removed the clips. The body was so hot the bucket of water was steaming. They had to wait until it cooled to remove the water bucket.

While everyone jumped in to help clean up the mess in the house, Hurricane took Jason outside. "Jason, buddy, we need the services of the clean-up team to take care of the trash here and at the barn. Can you find out who their associates are here in this area?" Jason and Hurricane had met the clean-up team in New York. They were professional and discrete.

"Sure, I can handle that," Jason replied. "I'll get right on it."

"Thanks, buddy. The boys in blue will handle everything else," Sam said, as Jason started toward his truck. Sam watched him go and was grateful to have friends like Jason that he could count on.

When everything had been cleaned up, they checked on Wallace again. There was no movement or heartbeat. Sidney Wallace, aka Michael Andrews, was dead.

Even though her pain and suffering were now a thing of the past, Connie still found herself tearing up. He had seemed like a kind and gentle man when she first met him, and he was the father of her children. She knew nothing of his past until after he was sent to prison. It came out that he had been a con artist and possibly a killer. That had not been hard for her to believe because he became a monster when he drank. Before she met Sidney, she would watch movies on television about women who had been deceived by men and think that women could not possibly be that naive. She was thankful that unlike some of the movies she had seen, this story had a happier ending. Not only was her daughter saved, but she had been reunited with her son. She had a wonderful husband now, and they were once again a full-fledged family.

Chapter Twenty-Three

Connie invited everyone over for a celebration party, and Raymond agreed to have it on Saturday, only two days away, so that Hurricane could stay and attend. Everybody was invited, including all of the law enforcement officers who had assisted in bringing an end to Sidney Wallace's evil rampage.

When Saturday arrived, Hurricane was up at four in the morning like always. This time, however, he had nowhere special that he had to be. It felt strange. Since his court date in New York, there had not been much time for him to just relax. Thinking back, he figured he had been on a special mission the past four or five years non-stop. It wasn't that he really minded it so much. It kept him out of trouble. Then again, with the kinds of missions he had been working, trouble always seemed to find him. He felt uncomfortable and worried that if he wasn't working he would get lazy.

Hurricane noticed the doorknob on his door was slowly turning. He quickly slipped behind the door. When the door was open far enough for the person to look inside, Sam heard Raymond say, "Where in the world can he be at this time of the morning?"

Hurricane quickly opened the door and almost scared the pants off of Raymond. They were both laughing, a little too loudly. Connie and Shirley came running out of their bedrooms. "What are you two doing?" Connie asked. "It's four-thirty in the morning. Can't you two wait a couple more hours to start playing?" They turned around and went back into their bedrooms.

"Yes, Sam, why are you up at this time of the morning?" Raymond asked.

"I'm just used to waking up early and getting a jump on life. I'm sorry if I woke you up. I'll be quieter next time," Sam answered.

"No problem, buddy, I guess I've just became a little soft with the married life. Someday you'll know what its like," Raymond predicted.

"No, not me, man. Not with the type of life I live, always having to look over my shoulder and make sure nobody's after me," Sam stated.

"You don't always have to be the Hurricane, Sam. You can always slow down and raise a family," Raymond said.

"I've been living this life for so long now that I don't think I could slow down and change," Sam responded.

"Who knows, maybe you'll meet someone who doesn't want you to slow down, or even to give up what you do. Then you'll have the best of both worlds," Raymond suggested.

"What woman in her right mind would agree to her husband traveling around all of the time and doing dangerous jobs that he may not come back from?" Sam asked.

"Love is a strange world, my friend. I know it sounds crazy, but there may just be that certain woman out there for you," Raymond replied.

"Fat chance, brother. It would be a miracle if I found a gal like that. Besides, you better get back to your woman before she gets mad at you, and me," Sam responded.

"Alright, Sam. I'll leave you alone, but I still think there's that special woman out there for you. Just promise me if you ever find her, you'll call me and let me know," Raymond said walking out of Sam's bedroom.

"You'll be the first one I call, but I still think you're crazy."

When Raymond left Sam's room, Sam decided to take a walk. He dressed in his sweat pants and tennis shoes and headed for the door. He figured by the time he returned everybody would be awake.

Sam couldn't believe how warm it was at this time of year. He had always heard that winters in Wisconsin were almost like New York. They lasted into late May and sometimes even the middle of June. He looked at his watch. It was exactly five-forty-five in the morning, but he figured the temperature was at least in the low fifties, perfect for a morning walk.

Sam decided to walk through Graceland Cemetery, figuring that since he had a lot on his mind, it would be a peaceful stroll. When he was about a half mile into his walk, he heard a scream. Looking up, he saw two men trying to take a purse from a lady visiting a grave. Sam ran over to the lady and told the men to leave her alone. They turned and warned Sam to stay out of it. Sam couldn't believe his eyes. They were kids, maybe fifteen or sixteen, but kids just the same. Sam decided to try once again, "Why don't you boys just leave before somebody gets hurt."

"Mind your own business, old man," one of the boys said.

"You'd better listen to my friend, old man, before we make you sorry you were born," his buddy said.

"I thought you boys might be smart and just leave this lady alone, but unfortunately, some people are born to learn the hard way," Sam replied.

"Man, since you really insist on playing superhero, we're going to cut you up real bad," the first boy said pulling out a switchblade knife at least four inches long.

"Now, just listen, boy, I don't want to kill you, and you don't want to end up dead, so I'm going to ask you one more time. Please, for your own safety, put the knife away before you really end up hurt," Sam said.

"Listen to you. You think you're some superhero? I don't see a suit of armor on you or any weapons. Maybe you can spin a web like Spiderman or stop a bullet like Superman. Which is it, man? Are you an ironman or a daredevil?" the boy asked in a sarcastic tone of voice that angered Sam.

"No, I'm none of the above. I'm a different kind of superhero, someone you've never heard about. Now, for the last time, please put down the knife, or I'm going to have to hurt you," Sam said in more of a stern voice.

"Hey, I think you're just a crazy old man trying to help this old lady. Maybe we'll let this little old lady go and kick your butt instead. Some superhero! What name do they call you, Grandpa?" the boy with the knife asked and smiled bright as he advanced toward Sam.

"I've tried to warn you, but some people always have to learn the hard way. Now, boys, I'd like to introduce you to the Hurricane," Sam answered. He twirled around so fast the two boys never saw his foot until it hit them in the head. They both staggered back and couldn't believe what had just happened. "Now, why don't you boys just walk away before someone has to carry you out?" Sam asked again and turned to help the lady up off of the ground.

"Look out!" the lady yelled as Sam kicked his leg back hitting the boy straight in the kneecap. There was a big pop and then all you could hear was a kid screaming.

"My leg, you broke my leg, you bastard." After he said that, he saw the look in Sam's eyes and tried to plead his case. "I'm sorry I swore at you, mister. Please! Please! Don't kill me."

"You apologize to this lady and get the heck out of here before I really get mad," Hurricane said.

They couldn't stop apologizing to the lady and Sam. The uninjured boy helped his friend up to his feet, and started toward the entrance of the cemetery. After the boys were gone, Sam asked the lady if she was alright. She gave him a kiss on the cheek along with a big hug as she said, "Thank you, young man. That was mighty brave of you."

"It was my pleasure, ma'am. I hope they didn't hurt you," Sam said.

"Sarah Jenkins is my name, son. I was just visiting my husband's grave. Alfred Jenkins. He passed away two years ago today from cancer. He was a good and kind man, just like you. He gave me two lovely children to remember him by. Unfortunately, our son Allen was killed in action as he tried to help free some hostages in Vietnam. He was given the Silver Star and Purple Heart by the United States Marines for his bravery. Here is his picture," she said, handing the photograph to Sam.

"I know him! I remember seeing him in one of the platoons. In fact, I think he was in our unit for a short spell. I never had a chance to meet him personally, but I heard from others that he was a terrific soldier. Always alert, always asking questions, and very knowledgeable. Then he disappeared, and I never saw him after that. I'm so sorry for your loss, Mrs. Jenkins," Sam replied. "And, by the way, my name is Sam Rufus."

"It's very nice to meet you, Sam Rufus. I think Allen is still by my side, and he sent you to help me today. Now, after what you told me, I'm sure of it, and it warms my heart so. I only wish that my daughter Janice would leave me be and find her own life. Since Alfred became sick with cancer, she has devoted her life to helping me. It's not that I don't appreciate it. She needs to find somebody to take care of her, or she may end up all alone in this big world. She has such a kind and gentle heart. I just hope she finds the right person someday." Sarah fished out a picture of Janice and gave it to Sam. "May I ask if you are married, Sam?"

When Sam looked at the picture, he couldn't believe how lovely she was. There was something about her eyes that showed warmth. Sam had viewed thousands of pictures of beautiful women, but something about Janice was very different. Just looking at the picture, he could somehow see her inner beauty as well. Sam was a bit choked up as he tried to hide his true feelings. How could he feel like this just looking at a picture? He tried to cover it up as he finally said, "No, ma'am, I'm not married. She's a very beautiful young lady, almost as beautiful as her mother. I wish I could meet her sometime. Maybe we will see each other again. I'll walk you back to your car to make sure you're safe. I wish I could see you home safely, but I have a party to get ready for, so I'll have to say good-bye for now."

"You're also a very beautiful person, Sam. I wish I could introduce you to Janice. She needs someone like you who cares about others. You have a way of bringing out the best in people. I can tell that. Janice and I have a party to get ready for as well, so if fate falls on us, we will meet again. If not, I hope you find a good woman and stop living a life all by yourself. You're too good of a man to stay single. Remember, behind every good man, there is a good woman. Someday you'll find her, Sam. I just know it," Sarah finished. Sam closed the door, and she drove off waving to him.

Sam looked at his watch and couldn't believe that he had been talking to Sarah for almost two hours. "Where did the time go?" he asked himself as he started walking back toward Raymond's place. When he arrived back at the house, Raymond was up and standing on the porch.

"I figured you went for a walk, my friend. Did you see anything interesting on your journey?" Raymond asked.

"If you have some coffee, I'll tell you the whole story of what I've been doing this morning, my friend," Sam answered.

Raymond opened the door as they walked into the kitchen. Connie poured them each a cup of coffee. Connie and Raymond listened to Sam's story. They both laughed when he told them about the two boys who tried to teach him a lesson. He told them about Sarah and her problems, and then mentioned something about Janice, her daughter.

Raymond couldn't hold back any longer. He had to ask. "What did you think of her daughter? She's some looker, isn't she?"

"She's more than good looking. She has a kind heart and an inner beauty I can see," Sam answered.

Chapter Twenty-Three

"Then you also met her as well?" Raymond asked.

"No, I just saw her picture," Sam answered.

"You mean you could tell all of that from just looking at her picture?" Raymond asked, kind of dumbfounded.

"I could see it in her eyes," Sam answered.

"Did you go and meet her then, Sam?" Connie asked this time.

"No, Sarah said they had somewhere to go today as well, so I told her that someday our paths may meet again," Sam answered Connie.

"Someday sounds so far away. Why don't you go and find her now?" Raymond asked.

"I don't even know where she lives. Besides, my life is too dangerous to get tied down to anyone. It wouldn't be fair to her, and I wouldn't want to put anyone through that kind of life," Sam answered.

"Sam, you might be surprised by what you find out if you just talk to someone. Don't judge anyone by what you might think they will say. I knew what I was getting into when Raymond and I first met. He was a gung ho Beret, and I loved him for it. He's still a gung ho Beret, and my feelings haven't changed one bit about him. I feel if we can do it, so can you," Connie said.

"I appreciate what you're saying, Connie, and that sounds too good to be true, but even if I wanted to talk to her, I wouldn't know how to reach her," Sam answered.

"If you had the chance, would you talk to her, Sam?" Connie asked.

"If I ever have an opportunity to talk to her, yes, I would talk to her. But what are my chances now? I don't even know where she lives," Sam answered.

"Sometimes the Lord works in mysterious ways. He may find a way to get you two together somehow, if it is meant to be," Connie said.

She waited for Sam to say something, and finally, after a few minutes, he mumbled, "I hope He forgives me for all of the destruction I cause when I'm on the job. If He feels I deserve such a chance, I will not let Him down."

Connie and Raymond both smiled at each other. They knew that Sarah and Janice were both invited to the party. They didn't want to tell Sam for fear he might chicken out before he had a chance to talk to Janice.

Chapter Twenty-Four

Sam looked at his watch. It was almost two o'clock in the afternoon. The guests would be arriving soon. Even though Sam had been around hundreds and thousands of people at one time, he felt a little uncomfortable for some strange reason. Maybe it was because at the other parties, nobody knew his way of life or how he made a living for himself.

Then his mind drifted to the picture of Janice. Could it be possible that such a girl might exist? Sam shook his head as that same old question arose in his mind. Would having a close relationship cloud his judgment on getting his job done? There are so many risks involved. If he slipped up, it wouldn't be just his life, but hers would be shattered, as well. Could she really accept this way of life and the uncertainty of his return that was a part of every mission? He could always give it up and seek a different kind of work, but this was all he had known since leaving the military. What else could he possibly do, and would he be happy doing whatever it was he found?

Sam snapped out of his thoughts as Connie yelled up to him that the guests were starting to arrive. He combed his hair back one more time and started down to meet their guests.

Walking out the back door, Sam couldn't believe the number of people who had already arrived. Most of the law enforcement officers involved in the rescue mission were there. He spotted U.S. Marshall Chester Mitchell and all of his gang. Many of the neighbors were also there. In fact, the neighbors on both sides of Raymond and Connie's house had opened up their backyards to help with the party.

Sam thought about how nice all of the neighbors were. He wasn't used to this kind of hospitality. Normally, it was a handshake or a kiss on the cheek, and he was on his way. These people were actually talking to him as if he were a real person. They even treated him like he was one of them. Every place he wandered to, he was approached by someone with a friendly conversation. Sam became aware that he needed to watch his language around these family-oriented people and realized that this atmosphere was refreshing.

Someone asked for the time. Sam looked at his watch and responded, "Four o'clock." He couldn't believe two hours had passed already. Raymond and Frank were busy cooking on the grills. In fact, they had several grills going at once. Sam approached them and asked if they needed any help.

"You're the guest of honor, Sam. You just relax. Ray and I have this under control," Frank said.

"All you had to say was yes, Frank. Besides, I don't mind getting my hands dirty. So just move over and let me help," Sam said sternly.

"Well, since you've put it so mildly ... okay. Climb aboard, soldier. But I'm warning you ... this is a tough crowd. If you burn these steaks, they'll horsewhip you," Ray said.

Sam, Raymond, and Frank were together once again, but now they were playing chefs and clowning around. They sang and flipped steaks on the grill. The ladies at the party brought the table foods—salads of all kinds, baked beans, cole slaw, hot dogs for the kids, brownies, cookies, some specialty cakes, iced tea, lemonade, and a variety of sodas. Sam told the guys they were wasting their time cooking because there was already enough food on the tables to feed an army just fine. They all laughed as the last of the steaks were almost ready to serve.

"Steaks are ready!" Raymond yelled. It was like a bull run as everyone ran up to grab some food.

Sam was waiting. He was never in a hurry for anything. His theory of life was: *Man who is always in a hurry most often makes mistakes*. He sat back and waited, watching the people in their processional around the tables. He happened to notice that a familiar face had come around the corner. It was Sarah, the lady he had rescued earlier that morning. Sam smiled, remembering what she had said about fate just a few hours ago. Then, as if he were dreaming, another person stepped around the corner. Sam was mesmerized. His eyes locked on the angel he had seen in the photograph this morning, and he suddenly couldn't breathe.

Sarah saw Sam standing alone in the corner. She took her daughter's hand and led Janice to him. Sam was cornered and couldn't help but stare at the beautiful creature walking toward him. It had been difficult enough just looking at her picture without acting like an idiot. What was he going to do now? He had no place to hide. He had never been scared of anything in his life. What kind of powers did she have over him? He had no choice. He had to face this. He just hoped he wouldn't screw it up. He glanced over at Raymond and Connie and saw them laughing at him. Sam had been set up for the first time in a long time, and his best friend did a great job this time!

"Sam," Sarah called, "I had no idea you and I were going to the same party today. It's good to see you, and I want to introduce you to my daughter."

Sarah turned toward her daughter. "Janice, this is the man I told you about who rescued me this morning. He is a very kind man and very quick on his feet. I had the impression this morning that he wanted to meet you, so I'll leave you two young people alone so you can talk."

"Sam, it is very nice seeing you again," Sarah said before walking away.

"I'm glad to see your mother is alright. She's a very extraordinary lady, and I really don't think she needed my help this morning. However, I was more than glad to assist her," Sam managed to say.

"I'd like to thank you for helping her. Sometimes she doesn't act her age. She doesn't think of herself as being old," Janice said, chuckling.

"She's a lot tougher than you give her credit for," Sam responded.

"My mother tells me you were a little tongue-tied this morning when she showed you my picture. Haven't you ever seen a girl's picture before? Maybe you were just trying to flatter an old woman's heart?" Janice asked.

Suddenly Sam felt his stomach start to tighten up as he tried to speak. After a few moments, he found his voice, "Janice, I have seen thousands of pictures of women before, but I must say, you are even more beautiful in person than in your picture. You have the prettiest eyes I have ever seen. I see a warm, loving person in your eyes, a person who is not only pretty on the outside but also just as beautiful, if not more so, on the inside. I hope you don't think I'm just saying this to get on your good side. I was also a bit nervous to meet you," Sam stopped and waited for a response.

Janice was blushing and very surprised at what she had just heard. She hesitated and then responded to what Sam had just told her, "Sam, forgive me. Now I'm tongue-tied. I have never heard such sweet words and such sincerity coming from anyone before as I have just now heard from you. I'm flattered but also confused. If you think so highly of me, as you have said, then why would you be nervous about meeting me?" she asked.

"Janice," Sam started, "I'm not as nice as your mother thinks. I have a mean side as well that she hasn't seen. What I do for a living may not be what you want from a man. I would be willing to try and change what I do, but I just don't know if I'd be as happy doing anything else. Someday, when I'm a little older, maybe, but right now, I don't think I could handle the change. I don't think it would be fair to put a woman through a life of not knowing when or even *if* I'm coming back from a special job," Sam explained to her.

"Samuel Hurricane Rufus, do you really think I'm so naive that I don't know all about you? I do read the newspapers. I know what you have done in New York, and now here. I know you must have a kind heart to be able to do what you do for other people. In fact, from what my mother told me, she's already caught part of your act in person. If you were the so-called 'killer' that you think you are, why did you let those two boys go? If you are trying to tell me that you would like to date me, just come out and ask me instead of going through all of this," Janice replied back to Sam.

"You are full of surprises. You know all about me, and yet you would be willing to go out with me if I asked you? I didn't think I would have a chance with you, but okay, here I go. Janice Jenkins, I would be so honored if you would go out on a date with me," Sam finally said.

"I didn't say I would go out with you. I just told you to come out and ask me," she said with a twinkle in her eye. Then, seeing Sam's face change, she added, "but since you've asked me so nicely, I'd love to go out with you."

"I love a person with a sense of humor, but why do you put me through so much torture?" Sam asked. "Come on. Let's get something to eat."

They both laughed as they sauntered up to the food table. Sam remembered what Raymond had told him earlier about meeting someone.

The only problem on his mind now was where he would call home if they became serious about one another. This place did seem to be growing on him. He decided to worry about that when and if that time came. After all, they had just met. But why did he feel like his stomach was tied up in knots?

After everyone had finished eating, Sam and Janice never had a chance to be alone. Sam was busy either talking or dancing with someone, and Janice was doing the same. They seemed to be the main targets for today's party. Just when they thought it was starting to wind down, Frank and Raymond set up a volleyball net. Raymond turned on the outside lights and announced that the games were about to begin.

They split up into six teams. Sam and Janice were on the same team but still couldn't talk to each other. They were busy having to plan out the team strategy. Each team played three games. The team with the most wins at the end was the winner. What they won was unclear, but it started out being tremendous fun. By the third game, they could hardly move. Just when they thought it was almost over, they discovered that Sam, Raymond, and Frank were tied for the lead. They would have to play a tie breaker.

Sam figured they were really trying to tire him out so he wouldn't have any energy left to go out with Janice tomorrow night. He might be a little older, but he was still in pretty good shape. At least, he was hoping he was. He would really find out tomorrow morning.

Janice was looking pretty good herself. Sam was watching her as she laughed and smiled with some of the other people. He couldn't believe the way he felt all warm inside just watching her. Could he really be in love? He had just met her. How could he feel this way about someone that he hardly knew? Even though he questioned his emotions, he couldn't help feeling happier than he had felt in a very long time. He decided to let his better judgment make the call. He would know for sure after their date tomorrow night. If he still felt the same way, and she turned out to be the real deal, he would be the happiest guy in the state of Wisconsin.

Chapter Twenty-Five

S am looked at his watch as he walked up to Sarah's front door and rang the bell. He was on time. Sarah opened the door and invited him inside. He looked around but didn't see Janice.

"She's having trouble with her hair. She'll be right down. Please sit down and relax for a few minutes. You look so nice all dressed up tonight, if you don't mind me saying so," Sarah said.

"I don't mind, Sarah. You look good yourself. Will you be alright here by yourself tonight?" Sam asked.

Sarah laughed and said, "You two kids just go out and have a good time. I have a friend coming over to play cards, and I'll be fine. Thank you so much for being concerned, but tonight is your night. I just hope everything works out for both of you."

When Sam saw Janice in the mirror looking at him, he turned and gave a loud whistle. She had on a low-cut red dress. He felt like the luckiest man in the world. "I just can't believe how beautiful you really are and why no guy has scooped you up yet," Sam said.

"If you're disappointed, we can always call it off," she said.

"You sure don't take compliments well, do you? I'm only trying to say how lucky I feel tonight having you by my side," Sam assured her.

Janice was smiling wide as she said, "I know what you were saying. I was just playing around with you, that's all. Now, let's get going, unless you want to spend the evening talking."

"As long as you're with me, I wouldn't care what we were doing," Sam responded.

"In that case, let's start out this night with a little miniature golf, shall we," she asked.

"Miniature golf? Well, if that's what you want, that's what we'll do. Your carriage awaits you, my lady," Sam smiled as they finally exited the house and went to the truck.

They were talking and laughing all the way to the golf course. It seemed like they had been going together for a long time. They both felt very comfortable and relaxed as they joked around with each other. They finally made it to the driving range and parked the truck. When they walked up to the counter and asked for a round of miniature golf, the man thought they were kidding.

"You two aren't dressed for no golf game, that's for sure!" he said.

"This beautiful lady here beside me wanted to play golf. How could I say no to a smile like this?" Sam said. Janice smiled from ear to ear.

Without saying another word, the old man gave them a ball and a putter. He chuckled as they exited to start their game.

Sam allowed Janice to go first. She sank the ball on the first hole for a hole-in-one. Sam knew he would never live this down, as it took him all four tries to sink his ball. When they were about halfway through the game, Sam noticed a carload of boys pulling into the lot. He watched as two of them exited the vehicle and headed for the little shed.

Sam had a way of smelling trouble. Feigning curiosity, he wandered over to the open area to check on the old man in the shed. He told Janice he'd be right back, that he had to check something out.

Janice said she would go with him in case he needed help. "Great," he thought to himself, "if trouble starts, I'll have to worry about her as well." Sam walked into the shed, and the one boy quickly lowered his hand. Sam knew he was holding a gun but continued to walk over to the counter.

"Hey, sir. How much are these bags of chips and a bottle of soda?" he asked.

Just as the man was about to tell him, Sam bounced the bottle off the head of the kid who was holding the gun, knocking him out cold. Sam ran after the second kid, and just as he turned the corner of the building, he was surrounded by five young men.

"Hey, mister, I heard you interfered in our business. For that, you'll have to pay the consequences."

"Just what are the consequences you refer to, my young friend?" Sam asked.

"First of all, I'm not your friend, sucker. Second, I want you to give us all of your money. And third, we have to cut you up a little for sticking your nose in where it doesn't belong."

"First of all, if you're not my friend, you must be my enemy. Second, you can kiss my ass. And third, why don't you and your little fairy friends leave before you feel some real pain?" Sam said, and then added, "Why is it that all of you young punks think that just because you are too lazy to work, everyone else owes you a living?"

"You must be crazy, man. There are five of us and just one of you."

"No, there are two of us. Now, get your butts out of here." Sam turned and saw Janice standing behind him. She had her dress tied up around her legs. Sam was startled and didn't know what to say. Not wanting to start a feud between him and Janice at this point, he put his attention toward the group of young men standing in front of him.

"Are you kidding me? You and your old lady against us? After we're done with you, mister, we'll have a ball with your old lady. We'll even let you watch, if you're still awake, that is," the leader said.

"I'm not his old lady yet, and as far as having a ball with me, you may not have any left by the time we get done with you. I'd suggest you listen to my boyfriend and leave while you still can, you juvenile slime bags," Janice said.

Sam watched his eyes and knew what was about to happen. Three of the boys came after Sam. The other two ran toward Janice. Sam spun around faster than ever and took two out as he hit them square in the chin with a roundhouse kick. The leader froze for a second, and Sam took full advantage. He was kicked with a powerful thrust that landed between his legs. He went down crying as Sam went to the other two who were just trying to get up. He brought two open hands together in a clapping motion, and hit both guys square on the ears, causing them to fall back down on the ground.

He turned his attention toward Janice and saw her beating the hell out of the other two boys. Sam had just found out that Janice was also well-schooled in martial arts. He leaned back and watched as she gave each one a roundhouse kick and connected in the same place as their fearless leader. The old man in the shed had called the police, but by the time they arrived, all five boys were on the ground begging to be arrested.

Sam walked over to Janice and asked her if she was alright. She nodded her head yes as they hugged each other. Just as they were about to go back to their game, they heard one of the police officers say, "Hey, you two, get back over here. We have a few questions for you."

Sam and Janice walked back toward them, and the old man came running out, "No, not those two. If not for them, I would have been robbed, maybe even dead. Who knows? They saved my life. It was those boys, plus one more in the shed."

"Just the same, we have to ask them a few questions," the officer said.

Before he could start his questioning, a sheriff's car pulled up.

"Sam, is that you!" Officer Kopecky asked as he exited his car. "What the heck are you doing here? Janice, are you alright?"

"Well, Officer Kopecky, Janice and I came out here for a round of miniature golf. As we were playing, these stupid boys tried to rob this poor man. We couldn't just stand by and watch that happen, so we decided to try and stop them. It's not our fault they were too dumb to understand the words to just leave," Sam said.

"You took on all of these young men all by yourself?" he asked.

"No, sir. I had a little help from this lovely lady here," Sam said.

Officer Kopecky chuckled as he said, "Sam, are you trying to tell me that this pretty young thing had a hand in this?"

Before Sam could answer, Janice interrupted, "Sir, I may have distracted them enough so that Sam could get them all by himself."

"Now, that I can believe, but you actually having a hand in bringing them down … that sounds a little fishy," Officer Kopecky chuckled.

They put the boys in the squad cars and took them to the hospital. Meanwhile, Officer Kopecky told the other officers to let Sam and Janice go. After all the fuss was over and he and Sam shook hands, Janice and Sam went back to their game.

"Wow, I'm impressed. Where did you learn martial arts?" Sam asked.

"My father was a retired colonel in the Navy. We traveled a lot until he became a colonel. He wanted Allen and me to be able to defend ourselves when he was away at sea. He trained us, or had Mr. Jameson, the martial arts expert, show us different techniques when he couldn't be with us. They taught us a little Karate, Jujitsu, and Taekwondo all rolled into one. And believe me, it has come in handy plenty of times, like today," Janice answered.

"You were very impressive, I must say. Not only are you a beautiful young lady, but you're also a tigress," Sam replied.

"Flattery will get you everywhere," she said smiling. "I saw a side of you that impresses me as well. Now I know why they nicknamed you 'the Hurricane.' You do move faster than anyone else I've ever seen."

Sam became quiet for a while, until Janice bugged him enough to open up and talk. She kept nudging him until he finally talked.

"How long have you known I was called 'the Hurricane'?" he asked.

"Are you kidding me?" she asked. "We do have a newspaper in this little city, and I do read magazines, too. I knew who you were the minute my mother told me what you did for her. She also told me how you reacted when she showed you my picture. I had to meet the man and see just how gentle he really was." She paused and waited for Sam's response.

"I guess you're a bit disappointed in what you've seen so far. I lost my cool back there."

"What I saw back there was a man who did everything he could to avoid what happened. They made the first move. You just countered. If anyone should be worried, it's me. I'm the one who lost control," Janice responded.

"Are you kidding? That was poetry in motion. We would make a great team," he said.

Janice smiled brightly as they continued their golf game. After Sam finally lost the miniature golf game, he took her to a fancy club on the beach for dinner and dancing. They had a live band that played everything from waltzes to rock and roll. They had a great time and couldn't believe how fast the night flew by. It was nearly three o'clock in the morning when they left the beach to call it a night.

Sam walked Janice to her front door and asked if she'd like to go out with him again that night. She smiled and said yes as she leaned up and gave him a goodnight kiss.

Sam was in seventh heaven as he drove back to Raymond's house. He kept thinking about the past nine hours he had spent with this tigress. He started smiling as he remembered what Raymond had told him, about how good a woman could make you feel.

When Sam entered the house, Raymond woke up. He eased out of bed and quietly went down the stairs to see who had opened the door. Sam heard him coming and was hiding on the side of the stairs. He grabbed Raymond's leg when he was two steps from the bottom. Raymond almost jumped back up to the hallway. Sam was laughing like crazy when he saw Raymond holding his heart.

"Damn you, Sam. You scared the hell out of me!" Raymond hollered.

Sam was laughing so hard he couldn't talk back, and Raymond eventually started laughing, too. Then he looked at the clock on the wall and started to smile wide as he asked Sam, "I guess your date was alright?"

"It wasn't just alright. It was pure heaven. Did you know she was schooled in the martial arts?" Sam answered.

"No, I didn't know. Did she tell you that?" Raymond asked.

"We had a little trouble tonight, and she was fantastic in defending herself," Sam replied.

"What? You two fought each other?" Raymond knew he had just asked a stupid question.

"No, you melon! We had a little trouble with five young guys, and she took care of two of them while I finished the other three," Sam responded.

"What? Am I hearing you right? Are you trying to say you might have fallen in love?" Raymond asked.

"I'm not sure what love really feels like, but my stomach feels like a bunch of butterflies are migrating in there. So if this is what it feels like to be in love, I guess you're right, my friend. Maybe I'm in love," Sam answered.

"Is this coming from the same person who, just the other night, told me he didn't think he'd ever find the right person?" Raymond asked smiling from ear to ear.

"Raymond, you knew she was coming over, and you set me up, but I really have to thank you. I only hope she feels the same way I do. I'll know for sure when we go out again tonight," Sam said.

"Well, I'll be a monkey's uncle. I hope it works out for you, Sam. You really deserve someone to be with who can make you happy. I wish you the best of luck. But for now, can I go back to bed? It's almost four in the morning, and I have a long day ahead of me tomorrow," Raymond said.

"Sorry, pal. Yes, I guess we should get some shut eye. Good night, brother, and sleep well," Sam replied and walked toward his bedroom.

Chapter Twenty-Six

Sam and Janice hit it off so well that Sam decided he would rent an apartment and stay there for a while. Raymond started to wonder if this was the real deal for Sam. He had only been seeing Janice for three weeks, and he was curious what Sam would do if a sudden call came through for help.

Meanwhile, Sam was able to find a job working with the Sheriff's Department. They made it perfectly clear to him, however, that they had to work by the book. Sam agreed, but Raymond knew if push came to shove, Hurricane would use force, no matter the consequences. He only knew one way to do his job, and that was to win, no matter what it involved.

After two weeks of silence, which was driving Sam a little crazy, a call came through of a burglary at the grocery store. Sam was behind the wheel, and he put the peddle to the metal. He was there within a few minutes. Just as he exited his car a figure of a man came through the door. Sam hollered, "Freeze! This is the Sheriff's Department! Put the gun down, and put your hands behind your head."

"Get away, copper, or I'll kill this girl!" he yelled.

"Where did that girl come from?" Sam thought to himself. "I never took my eye off the guy. Was I so preoccupied with the thief that I didn't see the girl? No, she has to be working with him. There is no way I could have missed her," he said to himself. He decided to play his hand and see what happened. He picked up his microphone and said, "Hey, buddy, how about giving me a break? I just started this job a few weeks ago, and my boss is watching me. Just release the girl and toss out your gun. I just couldn't live with myself if I had to kill you."

"You're pretty funny for a cop. You expect me to just give myself up without a fight?" he asked.

"I'm just giving you a chance to get out of this in one piece, my friend, unless you like pain, that is?" Hurricane said.

"What's your name, copper?" he asked.

"They call me 'Hurricane,'" Sam answered.

"I'm supposed to believe that you're that cop from New York? What do you take me for, a fool?" he asked again.

"Seems like you know all about me, partner, and I know nothing about you. That just isn't fair. By the way, do you know what I look like?" Sam asked.

"Yeah, I've seen your picture on television. I know what you look like," he answered.

"I'll tell you what, if you let the girl go, I'll come out in the open so you can see it's really me. Then you can give yourself up to me and become famous," Sam said.

"I'll let the girl go. But I'll have to think about giving myself up," he answered.

He released the girl, and she ran back into the building. Sam saw the glare from a gun handle in her sweater as the wind blew it back and the sun caught it. Then the gunman walked out into the open and was facing Sam's direction.

Sam kept his promise and came out to face the bad guy. His eyes never left the guy for a second. He saw the man's hand twitch and said, "Hey, pal, I didn't like what I just saw. Please don't be stupid, and maybe you'll be around long enough to see your girlfriend again. You know who I am. I can tell from the look on your face. So please don't think you can do what others have failed to do and draw faster than I can. Let's just talk about what's bothering you, and instead of you going to jail, you may just end up getting some help," Sam plead with the gunman.

"You're lying. They'll just put me in jail and forget about me," he said.

"No, you've done nothing except rob a store. If you surrender your weapons to me, I'll personally see to it that they get you help. Everybody goes through hard times, and some will try something desperate. I've been in that boat a few times myself before I landed this job. I can tell that you're not a bad person. You're just a little confused about a few things at this time. What's your name, pal?" Sam asked trying to settle him down.

"Tom. My name is Tom, and I already dropped my gun on the ground. So come over here and arrest me," he answered Sam.

"I'd like to do exactly as you say, Tom, except I can see that gun handle sticking out of your jacket pocket. I also saw your partner run into the store, and I haven't seen her exit yet, and yes, I saw her gun as well. So as soon as you call her out, and you both drop your weapons, we can continue this conversation. If not, my back-up will be here in a couple more seconds, and I'm not sure just what will happen then," Sam answered.

"I have to admit, Mr. Hurricane, you're good. You almost had me convinced to drop my weapon. However, I think I'll take my chances. I really don't think you're as quick as they say. I think I can outdraw you, and maybe I'll do just that and leave, with the money, that is," Tom responded.

Just as Hurricane was going to say something, three more squad cars pulled into the parking lot. All of the officers came out of their cars with their guns drawn. Sam motioned for them to ease up a little and then turned his attention back to Tom.

"Tom, as you can see, you have no chance to get away, so please, give up your guns. I don't want to see a good man like you get shot and possibly killed. Life isn't that bad, to just end it like this. Call out your girlfriend, drop your weapons, and we will help you. This is your last chance to surrender without consequences. If we have to force you to relinquish your weapons, I can promise you that you'll spend the next four to five years behind bars. I really don't think you want that, but the choice is totally yours. What do you say, Tom? We'll give you a minute to make up your mind. I hope you make the wise choice, my friend," Sam said, and then eased up a little, knowing he had back up to help him now.

After about thirty seconds, Tom called his girl out, and they dropped their weapons. Sam was so happy this ended without a gunfight. He wasn't really in the mood to kill anyone tonight. As he walked up to Tom and his friend, he extended his hand to shake Tom's hand. He nodded his head smiling, then he spun him around and said, "Sorry, pal, but I have to handcuff you for the ride to the station. It's nothing personal. It's just procedure."

When they arrived back at the station, Sam was called into the office. His Captain shook his hand and said, "I heard what you did. It took a lot of guts to get face to face with the perpetrator and talk him into surrendering."

"He was just under a lot of pressure, sir. He just lost his job after working there for five years. His wife is expecting a baby in a few months. He has no insurance and no other way to pay the hospital bills. He lost his head, along with his sister-in-law. They tried something stupid, and I hope the judge goes a little easy on them. There's no way they will be repeat offenders. I can guarantee you that, Captain," Sam said.

"Seems like he's not the only one who's made mistakes. I owe you an apology of my own, Sam," Captain said.

"Why would you owe me an apology, sir?" Sam asked, a bit confused.

"I jumped on your back a bit hard when you were first hired. I guess after hearing all those stories about you, I figured you were this hard-nosed guy who didn't like taking orders or going by the book. I guess I was wrong."

"As a matter of fact, sir, you were right about me. I've been on my own for so long as a private eye that I wasn't sure myself what I would do. I'm just glad this guy didn't force me to become what people have heard about," Sam said.

"You're alright in my book, Sam. I was wondering if you would like to work on my detective squad. I was told I could hire three more men, and I thought about you, with all of your previous experience. I was also going to ask Charlie Sanders and Mike Alders and see what they said, but I wanted to ask you first," Captain Morris said to Sam.

"Charlie and Mike seem like good candidates. They have a lot of time, and they've shown good instincts when I've worked with them. However, wouldn't it cause a lot of grief with asking me, considering I just started here, and there are others just as qualified for the detective job as I am?" Sam asked.

"Well, it's my decision, Sam, and I'm the Captain," Morris answered.

"Not to question your authority, sir, but could you ask the rest of the squad how they feel about it? If they agree, I'll come aboard your group," Sam responded.

"I respect that most about you, Sam. You always think of your fellow workers first. I will do as you ask, and if it works out, you'll be in." Captain Morris shook Sam's hand as he exited the room.

When Sam got back to his desk, he found a thank you note on his desk from Tom and his sister-in-law. They were thanking him for his help. He sat down and smiled brightly, hoping it would turn out the way he figured it would.

It was Friday. Sam's shift was over, and before he headed home, he called Janice and asked if she wanted to go out for dinner and possibly a movie or dancing. He walked out of the station with a grin from ear to ear. He was humming a tune as he walked up the steps and down the hall to his apartment. When he opened his door, he noticed his answering machine was blinking. That could only mean one thing—someone needed his help. He struggled in his own mind whether he should answer it or not. He decided to wait until after he took a shower and dressed for his date tonight.

Sam kept visualizing the call for help in his mind as he was getting ready to go pick Janice up. His curiosity finally got the best of him. He pushed the button and the voice came on. "Hello, Hurricane. This is Wayne Simmons. I'm calling from Las Vegas, and we could use your help. Please call me back." Sam jotted down the number and tucked it into his coat pocket. He decided to wait and ask Janice what she thought before he made the call. He couldn't believe how difficult it was. It finally dawned on him that he was really in love with Janice. The old Sam would have already been on the plane to Vegas. Then again, the old Sam didn't have someone he really cared about. Now he had a tough decision to make. Could he really walk away from a plea for help, if it came down to that. He would soon find out.

Janice noticed Sam wasn't himself as they sat down to eat dinner. The waitress approached and asked if they wanted drinks. After Sam and Janice made their order, she finally asked him, "Sam, what's wrong with you tonight? I've never seen you so quiet and distant before. Are you thinking of breaking up with me?" she asked with a bit of nervousness in her voice.

"Are you kidding me? You're the best thing that has ever happened to me," Sam answered.

"I'm glad to hear that. Now, what's the other problem on your mind?"

"I received a call today from a friend in Las Vegas. He needs my help, but I don't know what to do. I don't want to leave you," Sam said.

"Sam, I knew what I was getting into when I first met you. I'm not going to hold you back from what you do best. Besides, you will not have to leave me if I go with you, right?" Janice asked.

Sam looked up, surprised, "You would really go with me?"

"I've always dreamed about going to Las Vegas," she answered. "If you don't mind me tagging along, I'd love to go with you. Besides, didn't you say once before that we would make a good team? Maybe I could help you out if you get stuck with a problem."

Sam suddenly perked up and made a bold statement, "I'd love to have you go with me, but if things get too complicated, I want you to head back, no questions asked. I wouldn't want you to end up in any danger because of me."

"Agreed," Janice said, crossing her fingers behind her back. There was no way she would leave Sam in time of need. She figured the only way to make him understand that would be to prove it to him.

"I'll call my buddy, Wayne, when I get back to my apartment. But right now, I have a beautiful woman sitting in front of me that I need to entertain," Sam's smile was back, along with his sense of humor.

It was nearly three in the morning when Sam and Janice made it to his apartment. She wanted to be with him when he made the call. She was a bit curious just who this Wayne guy was. It couldn't be who she thought it was, could it? Sam pulled the piece of paper out of his pocket and dialed the number. Within a few seconds it was answered.

"Mr. Wayne Simmons, please. Let him know it's Hurricane," Sam responded. When he looked at Janice, her mouth was hanging open, and she looked surprised. "Yes, Janice, it's really him. I'll introduce you when we get there," Sam said.

Sam and Wayne talked for at least thirty minutes. Sam made it clear that he needed two tickets, and they would be there by Sunday. He had a few things he had to straighten out here first. After hanging up, he took Janice home and told her to pack for at least a couple of weeks. He'd be back to pick her up later tonight, and they would catch the last flight out tonight instead of Sunday. Meanwhile, Sam went to Captain Morris's house and explained the situation. He was instructed to be careful, and to report back when he returned. That was, if he still wanted the job. They shook hands, and Sam was off again.

Sam called Raymond and asked him to get his mail while he was gone. Raymond was a bit startled when Sam told him Janice was going with him.

Raymond broke out in a big smile as he told Sam, "You know, Las Vegas has a lot of chapels, in case it's getting serious with you two. I figure as long as you're there, why not get hitched?"

That was the first time it occurred to Sam that this might be the reason Janice wanted to go with him. He shook that thought from his mind. He had to concentrate on what he could take on the plane and what he had to leave behind. He had one more surprise stop to make before he picked up Janice. He had something he had to do, hoping it might just work out.

When Sam finally reached Sarah's house, he walked up and rang the doorbell. Sarah answered the door and greeted Sam like he was her son. She was so happy that Janice and Sam were dating. She made no secret about her wanting them to get married.

Sarah asked him about the vacation to Las Vegas they were taking together. It was apparent that Janice didn't tell her why they were going. Besides, why would they want to worry her? She had experienced enough pain in her life already, with her son and husband both gone from her life.

Sam was wondering what it would be like having someone with him on one of his trips. It felt a little strange waiting for a partner. Sam had never had a partner before, and he had never met anyone like Janice before either.

He had been in Las Vegas once or twice and had heard of strange things happening there, but he was unsure of just what people were talking about.

In less than an hour, Sam and Janice had picked up Raymond and were on their way to Billy Mitchell Field for their flight to Las Vegas.

"Hey, Sam, old buddy, could I use your truck while you're gone?" Raymond asked.

"Yes, Ray, you can use my truck if you want to. Besides, I can't take it with me, at least not this time. We are in a bit of a hurry," Sam said.

Raymond stayed with Sam and Janice until their plane left the airport. Under his breath, he said he could just see the headlines coming soon:

"Hurricane Strips Las Vegas."

Meet the Author

Joseph J. Cacciotti

Joseph Cacciotti grew up in Racine, Wisconsin, along the shores of Lake Michigan. His desire to write appeared early in life when his high school teachers encouraged him to write poetry and to become a journalist. His drive to write fiction grew stronger as he matured.

Joe made a promise to his friend and mentor, Harold A. Schink on his deathbed. Harold asked Joe to never stop writing. Joe has been faithful to that promise. In 2006, he published *Poems for the Heart*, fifty of his most talked about poems, and *Blue Collar Real Estate Mogul*, a biography based on true life experiences that he and his best friend endured as landlords in Racine and about a friendship that never stopped growing, even after death.

In 2009, Joe completed *Hurricane Cores the Big Apple,* the first in a series about Samuel James Rufus, an unconventional detective whose methods for getting the bad guys come close to crossing ethical and legal lines in his pursuit of justice. The first book, *Hurricane Cores the Big Apple*, reveals how Sam got the name "Hurricane." What has not been revealed yet is the dark side of the Hurricane, just how devious he can be. Every story reveals more about the Hurricane. At times, you might ask yourself who the real bad guys are in the story Sometimes, something more evil than the devil himself is called upon to balance off justice.

Joe lives with his wife Diane in Racine, Wisconsin. They have three daughters and a son. Joe continues to write the next books in the "Hurricane Sam Rufus" series.